MW00988272

Little Brats: Taboo A-Z
Volume 2

By Selena Kitt

eXcessica publishing

Little Brats: Taboo A-Z Volume 2 © 2015 by Selena Kitt

All rights reserved under the International and Pan-American Copyright Conventions. No part of this book may be reproduced or transmitted in any form or by any means, electronic or mechanical, including photocopying, recording, or by any information storage and retrieval system, without permission in writing from the publisher.

This is a work of fiction. Names, places, characters and incidents are either the product of the author's imagination or are used fictitiously, and any resemblance to any actual persons, living or dead, organizations, events or locales is entirely coincidental. All sexually active characters in this work are 18 years of age or older.

This book is for sale to ADULT AUDIENCES ONLY. It contains substantial sexually explicit scenes and graphic languge which may be considered offensive by some readers. Please store your files where they cannot be access by minors.

Excessica LLC
486 S. Ripley #164
Alpena MI 49707

To order additional copies of this book, contact:
books@excessica.com
www.excessica.com

Cover art © 2015 Resplendent Media
First Edition Fiona: January 2015
First Edition Georgia: January 2015
First Edition Hanna: February 2015
First Edition India: February 2015
First Edition Jenna: February 2015

Warning: the unauthorized reproduction or distribution of this copyrighted work is illegal. Criminal copyright infringement, including infringement without monetary gain, is investigated by the FBI and is punishable by up to 5 years in prison and a fine of $250,000.

Table of Contents

Little Brats: Fiona

She's a museum curator—an art-freaking-historian!" Fiona ranted, pausing only to slam her bedroom door. "And what does my dear old mother offer me as help for my art history paper? *Books!*"

She tossed three books onto her desk—the ones her mother had handed over when Fiona asked for help—plopping down in the chair at her desk.

"And now I'm talking to myself." Fiona snorted a laugh, glaring at the books.

She was bored to tears in art history—if she had to see one more painting by one of the so-called greats, she was going to scream—but she'd hoped for a little bit of hand-holding help from her mother, the self-proclaimed expert on the subject. Why she'd suddenly become delusional, expecting help from her mother, she had no idea. She chided herself for being surprised and threw open the first book.

"You've got to be kidding me," she hissed, looking at a book written in what she assumed was Italian, from her limited knowledge of the language. "What the hell am I supposed to do with this? Surely the woman owns the English translation. What the hell?"

She stood up and turned so fast, her short ponytail whipped around to slap her cheek. She'd rather be off working out at her stepfather's gym, getting high on endorphins and the sights of sexy, sweaty guys, instead of reading and writing about this anyway. Typical, all she'd gotten after asking for help was more trouble.

For her own benefit, she slammed the book closed before picking it back up again. For her snotty mother's benefit, she stomped as loudly as she possibly could in tennis shoes, down the path from her room to her mother's study. Unfortunately, that only worked well upstairs on the wood floors. Downstairs, on the way to her mother's office, it was all plush, white carpet that made the effort useless.

She stopped short when she reached the half-closed door, her mouth dropping open. Her parents were having sex. Her stepfather was fucking Fiona's mom, right at her desk, with the door half open! Had they no shame? They knew she was in the house!

As long as she lived, Fiona knew she would never understand why Bryan Nash, former Marine turned low-tech fitness gym owner, had married Aileen Muir, museum curator and uppity snob. It was the worst mismatch she could imagine. She knew her mother had seen the man's moneymaking potential—which came along with the fortune his family already had. That was a nice perk. But what did Bryan see in her mother? Fiona wondered.

Still fully clothed, her mother, a tall, curvy blond, bent over her desk. Her hands supported her, though they remained as stiff, as the irritated look on her face. Fiona saw her profile, lips pursed, eyes narrowed.

Her stepfather held her mother's shirt up at her waist, revealing only her taut ass, thigh highs, and silk panties, now decorating hundred dollar heels. Her mother spared no expense on herself. The only reason Fiona got the best when it came to her beloved yoga pants, sports bras and tennis shoes was because otherwise she'd be a total embarrassment to her mother.

Her stepfather's rock hard ass, tightening and releasing with each thrust, captured Fiona's full attention. He'd come to this sexual event nude. Completely nude. What the hell? She was right down the hall, for chrissakes! She knew she should turn around and walk away and try to scrub the memory from her mind with a good dose of brain-bleach, but it was Bryan's chiseled form that caught and kept her attention.

From the side, she got a decent, delicious view of his six pack abs and every other muscle making up his six foot two, one hundred and ninety pound athletic frame. Not that she hadn't seen him in workout shorts, all sweaty, a million times before, but this naked man plunging his hard cock in and out of her mother took things to a whole new level. A very wrong, very dangerous, unbelievably exciting level.

Curious, she squinted to see what she could of his erection. Slick and red, she saw enough to figure him well-endowed, wide and long. Her pussy pulsed suddenly between her thigh, a thick, hard throb, enough to make her stomach flip flop and her sex wet. Fiona wet her dry lips with the tip of her tongue. She was both disgusted and aroused by the display, two emotions she couldn't quite reconcile.

Then her mother turned her head. Fiona's heart leapt to her throat and she bit her lip to stifle a gasp. Her mother looked right at her! She saw the recognition in the woman's eyes, but she didn't overtly react. In fact, she didn't even flinch. All Fiona could read in her mother's blank expression was, perhaps, a hint of resentment in the tight line of her mouth, the glare of her eyes.

Could her mother possibly resent having to have sex with Bryan? But why? The man was a god among men—body and heart, actually. While both commanding and authoritative, she'd never seen him be anything but soft-spoken, patient and laid back.

Smart and down to earth, he let his emotions show, unlike most of the lunkheads he trained. Her mother, if she hadn't been so self-absorbed and judgmental, might have seen all of that, how lucky she really was to find herself such a catch.

Fiona's breath caught as her stepfather stopped. She saw the way his knuckles grew white where he now gripped her mother's hips, his arm muscles bulging and tense. Her shirt had unfortunately draped over his half in, half out cock.

"This just isn't working." Her stepfather grunted and withdrew. "What the hell is wrong with you?"

His words would have been accusatory from any other man, but he said them without a hint of malice. There was, instead, an overall sadness in his voice.

"Maybe you'll finally learn not to interrupt Mommy while she's working. Why don't you let Mommy take care of that hard cock for you so then you can leave Mommy alone," her mother simpered, both coy and cool as she bent to pull up her panties.

In a ladylike squat, knees together, her mother wiggled her panties up her legs and turned gracefully to put her husband's cock in her mouth. Fiona was utterly transfixed on Bryan's erection as it bobbed in the air, hard, long, and damp. The perfectly formed head made her mouth water and she ached to suck on him as well.

If it had been Fiona doing the sucking, there would have been no holding back. She would have gone to town on that length of pipe like she was trying to suck him dry. But Fiona's mother wasn't interested in getting sloppily throat-fucked. Aileen Muir placed her hands flat on Bryan's thighs, fingers splayed, almost pushing him away, as if she didn't want to have to touch him at all. Her position, the look on her face, everything, told Fiona that the woman was attempting to dominate him. Even the Mommy thing—Fiona was sure it had been meant to demean him.

What the hell? Fiona thought, her hand rising absent-mindedly to her lips.

She wanted so desperately to feel his hard cock pushing into her mouth, into her pussy, as she grew wetter, her pussy swelling and throbbing. She swallowed hard as her stepfather calmly, and with great restraint, slowly pushed her mother off his dick.

"Not tonight. I'm not in the mood for your games. I'd rather take care of it myself, thanks anyway," Bryan said softly before he turned and walked out of Fiona's sight.

Her mother turned directly to her, wiped off her mouth with the back of her hand, and then gave her daughter a sly smile. After adjusting her skirt, her mother sat down to get back to work. Fiona's stomach sank and she grew nauseous after seeing a man as great as her stepfather treated like that. By his own wife! Fiona's mother. Aileen Muir didn't deserve a man like that, Fiona thought, her hand clenching the book in her fist. She wanted to throw it at her mother's head.

The woman was a snobby bitch, always had been and always would be. Fiona had long given up even trying to obtain her approval or attention. She'd never accept, or even try to understand, her athletic daughter who would rather play with some ball and stick, as she put it, and work up a sweat, then hit the books and study something in a far-off ancient language.

"Well, is there something you want, Fiona?" Her mother's words were clipped. They dropped like ice cubes from her mouth.

"No, Mom." Fiona gave the woman her best look of disgust and loathing, although it was a complete waste of time, because Aileen Muir was looking at the papers on her desk and not at her daughter.

Fiona finally finished her art history paper, no thanks to her mother, and it was just going to have to be good enough for her college professor, because she wasn't wasting another minute on it. To reward herself, she went down to the kitchen to make a protein shake.

She opened the fridge to grab a Greek yogurt, trying to decide between a good run or some time with the weights to work out the frustration she had built up, sexual and otherwise, after seeing her parents together. As she shut the door, she heard the familiar sounds— deep breathing and slow, steady, methodical movements—of Bryan working out in their home training room. He'd built it long before he'd opened his own chain of gyms. That's where he'd created his low-tech fitness workout method that his gym chains were now known for, from heavy ropes to tractor tires.

She sighed, touching her mouth again, like a muscle memory, imagining his cock between them, making her lips swell with the hot friction of his thrusts. She put the Greek yogurt back and settled for a bottle of water with a slow smile and a lazy lick of her lips, going off to find him. The gym door was open and she saw his back muscles ripple through a set of sledge hammer swings. Although he moved at a fast, angry pace, he kept his form. She studied him while he didn't know she was there, drinking the man in with her eyes. How she longed to touch him and be touched by him. How could her mother resist? She didn't understand it.

Fiona leaned against the doorway, her chest full of pride and admiration for him, but her stomach clenched at the memory of her mother demeaning him, "taking care" of him as if he were just another job, a box to tick on a checklist. Her mother looked down on him, treating him like some failed project. Fiona knew how that felt, for sure. It made her want to go to him and the urge to hug him was overwhelming. Her mother's harsh judgment was swift and severe once she realized she couldn't make either of them like her.

"Hey, Sarge, you're puffing like a POG," Fiona joked, using a Marine insult, one reserved for non-marines, an acronym for "Person Other than Grunt." They often teased each other this way, but she wondered, after the incident with her mother, if he might take it badly. She waited for his response, holding her own breath.

"Really? Well, look who's talking, there, civilian. You obviously haven't even attempted to work up a sweat yet today," her stepfather playfully bantered back. His grin set her at ease.

"No, I have a college degree to earn, remember?" She rolled her eyes. "You were the one who insisted I do college, instead of come work for you, remember?"

"I did, and still do," he agreed, his mouth going all serious on her. She liked him better when he was smiling, laughing. He didn't do that enough anymore.

"Fine. Then don't complain when I don't get here on time. Not like..." she left off, not wanting to even bring up the subject of her mother or complain about the lack of help she'd received. She just wanted to work out with him, like they always did, and forget. "So, whatcha got for me? Make it good. I need to de-stress after that horrid, boring paper I just had to write."

"Fine. I challenge you to a medicine ball competition. Fifteen pounds, back and forth, see who can last the longest," he challenged as he rose to go grab the ball.

Before she could even agree, he tossed it at her, making the blue and white swirl of the plastic spiral through the air. Her hands out, she fought the instinct to protect herself from the weighted bullet hurling her way, and made a grab for it instead, her palms stopping the speed as she curled it into her chest in the proper form as he'd taught her. She'd held her breath so as not to let out a grunt when the ball hit her chest. Sometimes even his taking it easy could be a bit too much.

"Good girl," he praised, and her chest rose with her mood.

Her heart skipped a beat as he looked her over with approval.

"You thought I'd let you down, not coming in time?" she huffed as, with her elbows tucked in tight, she pushed out, sending the ball back to him.

"You never do. You give it your all when you get here, and regardless of how many times I win," he said with barely a hitch in his voice as he caught the ball. His arms flexed, but he pulled the thing into him as if it was nothing more than a child's toy filled with air.

"I hold my own, given you're ex-military, and I'm ex-debutante." She threw words back at him as he tossed the ball back at her.

"Okay, I'll give you…"

He'd left off as she caught the ball wrong, tipping her off balance enough that she hit her calf on a swirl of ropes on the floor. As she tried, with a fifteen pound weight curled in her arm, not to fall over, her stepfather took two long strides to catch her. Pulling her body close, he rolled them onto the floor. With her protected in his arms, she laughed as he grunted when they hit the floor.

Though his arms remained tight, she wiggled around to face him, more than aware of all his hard edges against her soft curves. While muscled, she had been given by birth the build of her real father, round and soft. While she had a nice rack and ass because of this, she had to battle, work twice as hard, for each muscle she built. She was surprised she could feel the large bulge of his cock against her stomach, even though he wasn't erect.

"Why do you let my mother treat you the way she does?" Fiona asked, the words coming before she could stop them.

"It's not her fault." Bryan's eyes widened only slightly before he shrugged in response. "I pursued her pretty hard. I knew she was out of my league, but... well, I wanted her."

Fiona listened, trying to understand. She couldn't fathom anyone wanting her mother.

"I knew we were different, but I didn't realize how much I was going to hold her back from the life she really wants." He sighed, his big arms tightening around her. "Your mother wants refinement, finesse. She wants a man she can take to dinners, parties, charity events."

"She wants a Ken doll." Fiona rolled her eyes.

"Maybe..." Bryan snorted a laugh. "But I was the one who let her down. I wasn't the fixer-upper she thought I'd be. I retired from the Marine Corps, like she wanted me to, but then I started the gyms. She thought it was a good idea. She supported me at first. But I think she figured, I'd get them started and then someone else could do the hard work while we just raked in the money. But I can't do that. I need to work for a living, not walk around tossing my money at people who feel obligated to call me sir."

"I don't think you need fixing up." Her brows furrowed as she listened to him take all the blame for her mother's horrible behavior. He took so much on himself. Feeling his body against hers made her lightheaded, pushing her nerves into overdrive. She had the urge to slither and slide her body against his and fought it.

"Sweetheart, you're young. You just don't understand. Aside from our obvious differences, I have a lot of energy, and a…" He cleared his throat, looking at her like he just realized she was in his arms. "A… voracious appetite for sex. Sorry. I know I probably shouldn't have said that, but it makes my point."

"That you're a horn-dog?" she teased, grinning. Damn, the man was as thick as a tree and just as hard beneath her. She was all too aware of him.

"Your mother, she wants the finer things in life, which includes a gentle lover," Bryan explained himself the best he could, but Fiona thought the ruddiness in his cheeks might actually be the flush of embarrassment. "What she got was some rough marine who never stops moving, wanting, and doesn't understand the concept of gentle."

Fiona shook her head, her nose wrinkling and brow furrowing at his words.

"She's champagne and I'm beer," he said. "She's the beauty and I'm the beast. She's frilly, expensive dresses worn to hobnob with the rich and famous, while I'm gym shorts in a concrete building filled with sweaty men."

When he put it that way, she could see his point. Although she preferred the latter to the former, to be honest.

"Your mother... she gives in to my needs from time to time. But she's grown to resent me for it. She tried to change me, I tried to change her. I thought, maybe we could meet in the middle. But... well, I failed for the first time in my life. I suck at wearing a suit and tie as much as I do sitting through a four course dinner."

"But, you're not satisfied either!" Fiona cried. How could he not see? Was he so blind? "She has no right to treat you the way she does!"

"You just don't get it." He sighed, shaking his head, moving to get up, but she clung to him, not letting go.

"Oh, I get it," she replied, giving in to her feeling as she slid her hand to wrap it around his cock, satisfied to find him already half-hard. Maybe having his stepdaughter in his arms was more exciting than he let on? "I get that you're being cheated out of what you need by a selfish, heartless woman."

His breath caught and he froze beneath her as she rubbed her hand up over his hardening cock. She was all too aware that he'd been in here working off his sexual frustrations after what had happened in her mother's study, and she took advantage of his need to prove her point. She kept her hand on the man's throbbing erection as the fingers of her other hand traced the ridges of his abs, his stomach bare and sheened with sweat. She followed the hills and valleys chiseled in his flesh, flicking her fingernail over his nipple, hearing his sharp intake of breath, feeling the resultant throb of his cock in her fist.

"Fiona," he murmured, place his rough hand, so big, over hers.

His touch tossed her over the edge. She wanted his hands. She wanted them roaming over her own curves, squeezing into her flesh. She moved her mouth to his, pressing her lips hard into his, using her flickering pink tongue along the seam of his mouth, seeking entrance. He groaned and turned his head, attempting to refuse her.

"I want you," she whispered, making her intentions plain, if they weren't clear enough already. "I would never dismiss you or treat you the way she does. You deserve someone who understands you, who gets you, who wants and loves you."

Her mouth found his again, and she felt him giving in. She felt the shift of his hips as she rubbed her hand up and down his cock through his thin shorts. She felt the way his mouth began to open, felt him responding, surrendering to the feeling. Oh, she wanted this man. She wanted him more than she'd ever wanted anything. She wanted to show him how sexy he really was, give him everything he wanted, wanted to match him thrust for thrust, climax for climax.

"Oh God, Fiona," he groaned, gathering her wrists in his hands. She liked that, liked feeling restrained by him. Their gaze locked and she knew her heart was in her eyes. He gave a low, pained sound, deep in his throat, but then instead of drawing her near, he pushed her away. In one strong movement, he brought them both to their feet before she even registered they were standing again. Cool air rushed over her tank top in the sudden absence of his warmth and she shivered, feeling her already hard nipples turning to beads of glass.

"No," he breathed, shaking his head. Then he said it again, more firmly this time. "No. No, this can't happen."

He let her go, hands now out in front of him, warning her to stay away.

"Your cock has other ideas." She nodded at the hard mass tenting his silky workout shorts.

She moved toward him again, grabbing his hands and lowering them to her waist, pushing up against him. Lifting to her toes, her body slid up his, arms snaking around his neck, until she could kiss him, rough, the way she knew he wanted it. And that did it. He began to respond to her touch, the way her hips began to grind against him, her mouth slanting across his.

His hands moved up to her round, perky breasts, and he squeezed, a low moan escaping his throat. For one breath-stealing minute, began to really kiss her back. His tongue probed, his leg lifting to tuck between hers, forcing her to ride the length of his thigh, making the seam of her shorts part her swollen pussy lips. The heat of her sex left a trail of fire as his thumbs grazed her nipples and she gasped, arching against him, showing him with every molecule of her being that she wanted him. She was more than willing to give him what he wanted—what he needed and craved. She needed it too.

"Fuck," he swore as they parted, shaking his head as he moved away. "No. Fiona, no. No!"

"You want me," she panted, trying to get at him again, but he held her at arm's length, his fingers digging into her upper arms. "I know you do! I'll give you what you want. Rough, just like you want it!"

"No." He said the word flatly, with no emotion, taking another step back and letting her go. "Go, Fiona. Get out of here."

"But…" She tried one more time, taking a step in his direction.

"Go!" He pointed at the door, but wouldn't look at her.

She finally gave up and ran from the room.

The next morning as she dressed, she heard a knock on her door. She knew the sound of her stepfather's heavy footfalls. She pulled down the tight material of her workout bra before she told him to come in. As he entered and saw her in her wearing just shorts and her bra, stomach showing, he averted his eyes, looking at the floor.

"Get dressed. We need to talk," he said to the floor, the command of his voice unmistakable.

He clearly meant business. She pulled a tank top quickly over her head, feeling the seams protest as she pulled it hard and tight to her waist.

"Dressed," she stated, turning her back to him as she packed up her book bag for her classes today, shoving in the damned art history paper, luckily protected in a folder from all her tossing and cramming.

"Fiona, please, we need to talk about yesterday, about what happened between us downstairs."

Her tears came, stinging her eyes at the memory, heat blotching up her face. She lost the battle to stop them in seconds. The first silent sob shook her, making her shoulders rise and fall. She dropped the last book in her hand and it hit the edge of the table before falling to the floor. She kicked the book, feeling her tears coming harder, realizing it belonged to her mother. She hadn't needed to put it in her book bag anyway, she'd just been packing things in, unseeing.

"Fiona, please don't cry." His voice was gentle as he placed his hands on her shoulders.

Not giving him time to even consider gathering her into his arms as he'd done before to comfort her, as her mother never had, she whirled on him. With two frantic swipes over her cheeks, she said the words through gritted teeth, "Just go."

"Fiona, no. We need to talk about this," he continued, undeterred by her tears or anger. "I know things have been stressful around here lately. We've all had a lot of changes—you starting college, your mom working on a new wing at the museum, me expanding the franchise of the gym and marketing my training system. But, that doesn't mean we can let our emotions get the best of us, and let something happen that will hurt all of our lives."

She just glared at him, biting her tongue.

"Our close sexual encounter…" He attempted a half-smile. "It was a mistake, sweetheart. It can't… it won't happen again."

Fiona, looking everywhere but at him, zipped up her bag and threw it over her arm, only snatching up her jacket as she brushed by him.

"I'm going to be late for class." She fled, not wanting to face him, or what she was feeling. Not now, not ever.

Fiona lugged her suitcase to the garage to throw it in the SUV. Bryan stood at the hatch, rearranging skies and poles and other gear for their family trip to Lake Tahoe. He smiled as he approached. Funny, how things had gone back to normal so fast. It had been months since that day in the gym. Neither of them had talked about it again and she told herself she was glad. It had been a mistake, like he'd said.

"So, where're mom's ten bags?" Fiona joked as he reached to relieve her of her burden.

"Your mother'll be flying out to meet us, hopefully sometime tomorrow." He tossed her bag into the SUV. "She got a call from the museum, some fire she needs to put out before the next show. They can't do anything without her, you know."

"Oh, I'm well aware of that fact. She tells me all the time." Fiona laughed and rolled her eyes. "So, maybe we can do one of those back country runs we always talk about, but somehow my mother guilts us out of?"

"Sounds like a solid plan." Bryan smiled at her.

They were still workout buddies, if nothing else. Fiona hadn't been looking forward to the long drive alone with him, afraid forbidden topics might come up, but they didn't have time to talk. The snow grew worse the further they got. Bryan was a good drive, but his knuckles were white by the time they pulled into their resort at Lake Tahoe.

"This is really bad," Fiona let out her pent-up breath as he parked. She hadn't been sure they were going to make it at all, as the roads grew increasingly harder and harder to navigate due to all the snow.

"Well, at least we know they've got snow." Bryan opened and closed his fists like they ached from holding the steering wheel so hard.

"Let's go skiing then." Fiona hopped out of the car.

They got in a short run before they closed down the slopes. Who ever heard of too much snow to go skiing? But they were having blizzard conditions by late afternoon and there was nothing to do but sit in the room and stare at the fuzzy static of the satellite television. Her stepfather looked out the window, but everything was white.

"I still can't get any reception." He sighed, pocketing his phone. "Your mother left me a message. Her flight's been delayed. Weather Channel is predicting a good twenty-four hours or more before the airports can open back up."

"Some vacation." Fiona sighed, punching buttons on the remote, hoping to find something, anything, that wasn't static.

"Why don't you start dinner while I go grab some wood?" he suggested, shrugging his coat on.

"Okay," she agreed, grateful they'd stopped on the way in to grab some food at the local grocery. "The steaks we brought okay?"

"Sounds fantastic," he said as he opened the door, the world a flurry of white.

Bryan came back, red faced and sweaty, carrying a huge stack of wood that would have buckled the knees of most men. She smiled as she continued to chop vegetables in the kitchen. Their room had a nice, open feel. From the granite counter where she worked, she could see the wide expanse of the living room, all white with a plump couch and plush carpet, looking even more pure and clean given the wood around the fireplace, the same rough cut that made up the rest of the furniture. It had an elegant, rustic feel, a nice compromise between her mother and stepfather.

He deposited the wood, throwing a few logs onto the already roaring fire, and told her he'd only be a minute as he went into his bedroom to try Fiona's mother again. She finished putting together the salad, thinking about their drive. It had been tense and nerve-wracking. Her neck was still tense and she shrugged her shoulders, rolling her head, trying to work out the kinks. But that wasn't the only reason she felt so tightly strung. It was being alone with Bryan. They hadn't been—ever again—not since that day. They still worked out together, but Bryan took her with him to the crowded gym with him. If he found her working out in their home gym, he'd just wave and say he was going for a run—alone—if she invited him in.

She supposed she couldn't blame him. She'd overstepped her bounds and she knew it. He wasn't the type of man to cheat, even if he wanted to. It was one of the things she admired about him. They'd managed to repair their father-daughter relationship over time, burying their feelings, that incredible urge to let nature take its course. She put all her frustrations into working out, and he did too. It had made them both tight, toned and incredibly fit.

Fiona glanced up, listening. She didn't hear him talking on the phone. Where was he? She didn't want to put her special o olive oil and balsamic vinegar dressing on the salad until they were ready to eat, so she put it aside and went to check on him in his room.

"Bry?" The door was cracked, but there was no response.

She pushed the door open. Bryan's iPhone was on the floor, about a foot beneath a phone-shaped gouge in the drywall. The screen blinked through cracked glass. Walking into the empty room, she picked up the phone, seeing the voicemail page up. Trying to hit the play button on the now -distorted screen, her mother's voice floated into the room, emotionless as usual.

"I'm not coming, and I won't be here when you get back. I've filed for divorce and will be moved into my new place by the time you're back from your trip."

She didn't even mention me, Fiona realized.

Her attention was drawn by the sound of running water coming from the bathroom. She poked her head in and saw him through the frosted glass of the huge two-person shower. With his palms against the wall, head down, defeated, the water streamed down his naked shoulders. She followed its path down his strong, broad back, his naked backside and powerful thighs.

She'd never seen the man bow his head, not to anyone, in any situation. Her stomach dropped. She didn't know how her mother could be so stupid as to give up on a man like him. Never having seen him even close to broken, she felt compelled as she walked toward the shower and stepped in, clothes and all. As if possessed, she moved to him. When she touched his back, his forehead fell to touch the wall. She felt him shake as he let out a long, deep breath—whether it was anger or sadness, she didn't know, but she swore she could feel him sobbing, screaming inside.

Running her hands through the stream of water, over the tense muscles of his back, she welcomed the heat of the spray that soaked the thin t-shirt and yoga pants she'd put on after her own shower. Moving into him, letting her breasts, her stomach, press into his back, she reached around to his stomach. She ran her hands over his chest, splaying her fingers to fit over the huge, hard mounds of his pecs.

When he didn't move, she ran her fingers down over his six pack ABS, appreciating each dip and each rise as she felt him shudder. By the time she reached down to wrap her fingers around his cock, he let out a low cry-like moan that tore from his throat. She slid her fist down his shaft until the side of her hand thumped against his balls, hearing him emit a low growl.

He turned on her then, so fast she had no choice but to move a step back lest she be thrown to the ground. Something burned in his eyes. She saw it even though he blinked from the spray of water. Stepping and reaching at the same time, he put his hands on her hips and spun her around. She sucked in her own deep breath as he peeled down both her pants and panties in one swift tug. She managed to step out of the material cuffed around her ankles as he bent her over, pushing her with one hand heavy until her palms flattened against the small bench along the side of the shower.

He used a knee to part her legs, widening her stance. Thankfully, he had a firm enough grasp on her that she couldn't slide anywhere. With one hand, he pressed his fingers between her folds, she guessed to check her for wetness. Finding it, he growled again, the sound fierce, primal, as his fingers disappeared, replaced by his hard cock pressing against her opening.

Letting him just take her, neither of them said a word, only grunted and groaned, raw, primal cries as he forced his way into her body, hard, making her stomach coil from the welcome invasion. He stretched her as no man ever had before, and she rode the glorious touch of pain as her inner walls adjusted to his girth. His fingers dug in. It only took a few thrusts before he managed to bury himself as far as he could, balls-deep inside her.

In and out, he pounded her, swift, jerky movements, the tip of his erection hitting that soft spot inside of her that made her see stars. Her stomach contracted, fluttered, contracted again. Their breath came in harsh pants as she squeezed him, the muscles in her pussy just as toned as the rest of her. The steam rose up around them, the hot water streaming over their heated flesh, the wet smack of their bodies, the hard, driving sound of their sex, filling the small space, echoing off the tile.

"Fuck me harder!" Fiona panted, arching up to meet him, onto her toes, grinding her hips into his. "Harder! Fuck! Harder!"

She wanted more. He was so fucking strong, grabbing her hips, the deep throb of his cock buried in her womb again and again, but it wasn't enough. She wanted the full blast of him, every bit of energy and motion he could muster.

"Oh baby, take it. Take my big fucking cock!"

"Yes!" she gasped at those dirty, naughty words. She wanted to take it, to take all of him.

He reached around and grabbed her wrists, pulling them behind her back, forcing her breasts to jut forward, her shoulder blades folding like wings as he rammed his dick home. He pulled hard, hands wrapped around her wrists, using her whole body as leverage, working his cock between the wet, swollen, aching folds of her flesh.

"Give it to me!" She moaned, writhing, squirming back against him, nearly bent in half now, her cheek against the bench. "Give me all of it, Daddy! Take that pussy! Make it yours!"

"Holy fuck," he groaned. She was afraid, at first, he might stop when she reminded them both exactly what was happening here, but her words had the opposite effect. If she thought she was being fucked hard before, she was in for a surprise when he whirled her around and lifted her in his arms as easily as if he were picking up a child.

"Daddy!" Her eyes widened as he thrust up with perfect aim and impaled her on his pole, the head of his cock buried so deep she thought she could feel it somewhere near her navel.

"Did I hurt you, baby?" He had her pinned to the tile, spread like a butterfly.

"No!" She wrapped herself around him, arms and legs, rolling her hips, feeling his dick hitting every part of her inside.

Fiona slipped a hand behind his neck, kissing him deeply, sucking on his tongue, drawing it into her mouth. He grunted at her response, beginning to thrust, which made her moan and break the kiss just so she could take a breath.

"That's so good," she murmured, biting at his thick neck, the solid hunk of flesh of his shoulder. "Your cock feels so fucking good!"

"Oh baby, you're so tight," he moaned, his hands gripping her ass as he fucked her higher and higher up the wall. "So motherfucking tight…"

"It gets tighter," she assured him, squeezing her muscles, making him cry out as if he were in pain. "And tighter."

She did it again, harder this time, satisfied by the deep, guttural growl he gave her, the faster, deeper thrusts, completely out of control. He fucked her like an animal, driving her higher, higher, literally and figuratively. Her back slid up the tile as Bryan stepped up onto the shower bench. Fiona's head nearly touched the ceiling and she swore he was going to fuck her into oblivion, all the way to the heavens.

"Oh baby, I can't stop it," he groaned when he felt the first flutter of her pussy around him, her climax imminent. "I'm going to come!"

"Yes!" she cried, teetering on the precipice. "Come for me, Daddy! Fill me with all that hot fucking cum! I want it—give it all to me!"

He let out a low groan, shuddering into her and burying himself to the hilt, grinding deep, their bodies stuck together in a quivering, wet mass. Fiona's orgasm made her tremble, her ears ringing, pussy snapping around his throbbing cock again and again, milking every sweet blast of his cum from his tightly-drawn-up sac. They both cried out in unison, riding the frantic wave of pleasure, blooming fast and then exploding deep within. As she came back down, tiny pulses of pleasure still shaking her to her core, Bryan slowly let her go, their bodies sliding down the tile until he was standing, still holding her close. .

His scruffy cheek against hers, he pulled her into the spray of water. Sitting on the floor, his arms around her, he pulled her down onto his lap. Yanking her soaked t-shirt from her, he then stripped her of her bra before curling her into his arms under the water. Their eyes forced closed by the warm flow of water as her head came to rest against his chest, he kissed her cheek as he rocked her. Having moved so swiftly from rough to loving, she took a moment just to feel him so close, skin to skin.

"I don't know whether to apologize or thank you," he said, his voice low but soft in her ear.

"You don't have to do either." She snuggled into him, luxuriating in his naked flesh. "I've wanted you for so long. You mean the world to me—you raised me, loved me, when my mother couldn't."

"Oh, sweetheart." He kissed her forehead, sighing. "I'm so sorry. I shouldn't… we shouldn't…"

"Don't you dare!" She pulled back to look at him, glaring. "Don't you dare reject me again! I can't… please… I know you want me. I know you love me. I can feel it."

She put her hand on his chest, over the slow, steady beat of his heart. Resting, it was as low as sixty beats a minute. The man was in better shape than some teenagers she knew.

"Fiona, I…" He shook his head, meeting her eyes, and she saw what she wanted there. If only he would say it. "Oh hell. Yes, sweetheart. Yes. I love you. I want you. I do. I've denied myself so long…"

"You don't have to deny it anymore." She pressed herself fully against him, straddling, feeling his cock, still slick and half-hard, trapped between them. "She might not have wanted you, but I do. I can take it. Everything, anything you want to do to me, I can take it all."

"Anything?" He raised his eyebrows. "That sounds like a challenge, little lady."

"It is." She stood up then, completely naked before him, round breasts heaving, stomach tight, ass clenched. "Take me any way you want, wherever you want, however you want. Not only can I take it, but I *want* it. I *love* it. I'm not a pussy and you know it. I'm not a little girl anymore. I'm a grown woman and I can match you, Sarge. So yeah, it is a fucking challenge."

An odd sound, a grunt mixed with a growl, more animal snarl than human noise, erupted from him his throat as he stood, making her instantly feel like prey.

Both fully exposed and unashamed, facing each other, he roughly grabbed her arm and led her from the shower, hitting the button that shut the multi-nozzled showerhead down.

He threw a big burgundy towel at her. Unsure, unable to read his face, she took it and began to dry, following his lead as he did the same.

"You think you can take me?" he asked as he towel-dried his now-growing erection. "You've no idea what I want—my appetite, my needs."

"I have some idea." She nodded toward the shower where they'd just fucked like animals as she roughly moved her towel over her breasts, mimicking him. "And I think you underestimate me."

Letting the towel drop to the floor, she slid her hands over her stomach, moving one to her breast, the other to her mound. He watched, a light in his eyes, as she squeezed fiercely, pinching her clit with one hand, her nipple with the other.

"Not only can take it, I *want* it." She hissed the words this time, her voice hitching as the pain turned to pleasure, making her tremble with her need, to be taken by force. No man had ever taken her the way Bryan had. It hadn't exhausted or sated her. It had simply made her crave *more.*

"Game on then," he growled, right before he scooped her up in his arms.

With long strides, he walked them into the bedroom and literally dropped her onto the bed. Her body hit the mattress and bounced, shaking her tits just slightly as she held her ground, returning his steely stare. His erection jumped when she let her knees fall open to him, a dare. He pounced, big hands gripping her inner thighs, pressing her into a full, wide open stretch, so far she felt the burn, a taut ache.

She let out a moan, but it wasn't a cry of pain, as he lowered his mouth and literally began to eat her. His tongue swiped flat along her folds—she was hairless all over, completely waxed to avoid chafing when she worked out—sometimes trying to push inside her, sometimes licking up her juices. He sucked her wet, swollen pussy lips into his mouth, biting, getting rougher with her, encouraged by her blissful mews and howls of pleasure.

He kept her spread wide open, knees out to the side in a parallel stretch. Her body began to sing, her clit throbbing. He seemed to know what she wanted as he sucked it into his mouth, spanking it with his tongue. Fiona was stretched so tightly she felt like she might snap, like a guitar string wound too tight.

"You like that?" He stopped his clitoral tongue-abuse for just a moment to ask. "You want more!"

"Yes!" she cried, squirming under the press of his hands. He had her pinned, she couldn't move. "Oh fuck, yes! Lick me! Lick my wet pussy!"

"Mmmm." His eyes lit up as he backed away just slightly, his hands sliding up to her knees. Her thighs burned from the stretch she'd been in for so long. "You want my mouth?"

"Yes!" she panted, arching her hips up toward him. He stood beside the bed, looking down at her. "More! Please!"

"Meet my mouth." He leaned in, tongue lashing, parting her swollen labia, back and forth. "Come on. Higher."

Fiona's hips rose to meet his mouth as he moved up a little more. Then a little more. She moaned, rocking up and up, straining, until her hips were as high as they could possibly be, her whole body tense and trembling.

"Fuck! More!" She growled. "Lick it!"

"Backbend," he instructed. "Full backbend. Do it. Now."

"Bryan!" She groaned, but she arched and bent her elbows, planting her hands on the firm mattress and rising up into a full arch, her wet hair grazing the bed.

"Good girl!" he murmured his appreciation, and then he showed it to her, hands gripping her ass, helping keep her up, as he fastened his mouth over her mound. She moaned and shuddered, body drawn taut, the blood rushing to her head in its upside down stance—what blood she had left circulating that wasn't gathered in the swollen folds of her sex.

Bryan's mouth clamped around her, sucking and licking and biting all of her, relentlessly until she broke. Finally, finally, her climax ripped through her and she screamed as she came, her hips pushing against his mouth, fucking his face, until the last contraction had passed. She ached all over and her body threatened to collapse, but Bryan kept his hands on her ass, kneading her taut flesh.

"Don't move."

Oh fuck. Her head swam, black dots appearing in her vision, but she stayed in the backbend, her limbs trembling.

"Jesus Christ, you're beautiful." He moved to stand at the end of the bed, looking at her, head cocked, his erection throbbing in his fist as he pumped it up and down.

She fought the urge to collapse, left herself like that, upside down, surrendered and completely vulnerable to him.

"I told you I could take you," she walked her legs closer to her hands, increasing the stretch even if it made her feel dizzy. "You need someone like me."

"Come here." Bryan grinned as she slowly, gracefully unfolded herself, sitting up on the edge of the bed to look at him. She was face to face with his cock, and it made her mouth water.

"I said, come here." He grabbed her and threw her over his shoulder, giving her ass a hard slap as he walked them into the living room. She squealed and laughed, but she wasn't laughing when he plopped down onto the couch.

She'd barely caught her breath when he pulled her down onto his lap. As she straddled him, his cock came to rest, heavy against her stomach. Inspired, she scraped a nail down over it. He bucked and hissed, grabbing a handful of her hair. She, in turn, grabbed his cock, giving it a few harsh pumps before she lifted herself just enough to push him into her wetness.

"Damn, girl." He gave her hair another tug.

She smiled, moving up and down on him, wanting him, needing him, deep inside her again. Her hands went to his shoulders for support and his moved to grab her breasts. Squeezing and kneading, sometimes pinching her erect buds, the sensations shot straight from nipples to her throbbing clit. She moved her own hand between her thighs, pushing the pads of her fingers to stroke that aching little nub of flesh.

"Fucking beautiful," he said as he watched her touch herself, her flat stomach tight, not an ounce of extra flesh on her. She saw him watching her circle her clit, right at the top of her bare cleft. She was wet from his mouth, her clit sensitive, but she still wanted more.

"Let me." He pushed her backwards, hands sliding down her ribcage, her waist, pressing back and back until she was parallel to the floor, stretched out over his legs, his cock still buried deep inside her. Her head rested against the coffee table and she had to use all her core muscles to stay in that position as his fingers spread her, thumb circling her clit.

But she didn't just stay there. She grabbed the couch cushions in her fists for leverage and rolled her hips, It wasn't easy in this position, but she managed to grind herself against him, round and round, satisfied when she heard him moan and pump his hips up in response.

"You little minx." He rubbed her clit back and forth, around and around. "I'm going to make you come for me, sweet girl."

"You better," she gasped, biting her lip and seeing stars. "Oh fuck! Ohhhh yess!"

"Like that?" He circled and circled, the same motion, faster, faster. "You like that, baby?"

"Yes, Daddy!" she cried, arching and letting go of the cushions so she could squeeze her nipples, sending shooting sparks of pleasure to her clit. "Ohhh yes! Daddy, I'm going to come for you! Make me come all over your big cock, Daddy!"

"Do it!" he cried, spanking her pussy with his fingers now, grinding into her clit with his palm. "Come for me! Come, baby! Come for Daddy!"

That did it. Her orgasm shook her so hard the contractions tore through her stomach, making it ripple and writhe as she sat up, wrapping her arms around his neck, riding the waves like a surfer, fast and hard, completely balanced even as everything was out of control. She came all over his engorged cock, her pussy tightening again and again, making him moan and grit his teeth.

"Daddy's going to fuck you so hard, baby girl!" He let out a low growl as he removed her from his cock and set her on the coffee table like she weighed nothing at all.

She sat there, dazed, breathless, shaking her head to try to pull it together. Her climax was still shuddering through her.

"On your knees, grunt," he commanded, reaching down to smack the side of her hip. "Table. Now."

She moved fast to obey, grabbing a pillow to make it a little easier on her knees, balancing on the coffee table on her knees.

"Put that ass up into the air," he barked.

She arched her back, pushing up her ass only to have her round cheeks connect with his rough palm. A spark of heat rippled through her.

"That only makes my pussy want your cock more," she said with a wiggle, pushing her reddened ass closer to him.

"Another challenge?" he grumbled as his hand hit her ass, big enough to hit both cheeks, rough enough to cause a hot friction and a nice sting.

She stayed strong, barely moving each time he spanked her. Only a few smacks later, he moved his arms around her waist, pushing his erection deep inside her. God, the man had perfect aim. Keeping her ass slightly raised with one arm under her waist, he rode her even harder than in the shower, if that was even possible. His cock plundered, taking what it wanted, and so did he. There was no holding back, just a complete letting go.

Fiona arched her back, pussy throbbing as he pounded deep, deeper still, his hands gripping her hips. He liked this position and so did she. She loved the feeling of him behind her, the slick smack of their bodies as they fucked, the way he could get as deep inside her as possible. But she wanted more still. She wanted to see him, watch his cock impale her.

"Wait, wait!" she cried.

"You give up?" he snorted, sounding smug.

"No." She snorted, shifting forward and sliding off his cock. She climbed down off the coffee table and stretched out on the rug in front of the fire, reaching her arms out for him. "Come here!"

"What do you want?" He knelt between her legs, his eyes bright in the firelight as she grasped him in her fist, pumping him fiercely.

"I want to watch you fuck me, Daddy."

He groaned at her words as she aimed him, lifting her hips to meet his thrust as he slipped into her wet hole. She welcomed him with a snug, heated squeeze, arching her back, showing him her body in the firelight. He looked down at her, his gaze sweeping over her rounded breasts, nipples hard, pursed, belly tight and smooth, the dip of her waist, hip bones like wings, a sweet V leading to the bare crest of her mound.

Fiona gripped his biceps, digging her nails in as he began to move again. She lifted her head so she could watch her stepfather fuck her, his shaft thick and red, swollen with the blood pumping through his veins, parting the pink labyrinth of her sex. He stayed propped above her, watching too, the place where they were joined. Each driving thrust brought them closer and closer to climax.

"Oh Fiona, you feel so good," he groaned, moving faster, deeper. "You make Daddy's cock so fucking hard."

"I know." She licked her lips. "I love your big cock in me, Daddy. I've wanted it for so long. So very long."

"Oh fuck," he whispered, biting his own lip. "Look at that. Look at Daddy's cock going into your hot little pussy."

"Mmmm, yes," she agreed, looking down at his shaft disappearing between her legs, and then lifting her eyes to meet his gaze. "I love it. I love the way you fuck me."

It wasn't rough now, but tender, and still, so fucking hot. The friction building between them rose higher and higher as they panted, working for it together. She'd spent hours working out with this man, pushing her body to its limits, and here she was doing it again, with a far bigger payoff than an endorphin rush.

"Are you Daddy's girl." His eyes searched hers. "Are you mine, Fiona? Say it!"

"Yes!" She lifted her hips to meet his, reaching down to feel him entering her. "I'm yours, Daddy. I'm your girl. My pussy is all yours. Take it. Take me. Oh God, Daddy, please, make me come for you!"

Her clit throbbed under her fingertips as he groaned and redoubled his efforts, hips moving all on their own, without thought or consciousness. They were joined together, two becoming one. They weren't just man and woman anymore, father and daughter, they were something primal, animal. They weren't having sex, they *were* sex. They weren't fucking—*they were fuck.* Pure, raw, animal fuck.

"Fuccckkkkkk!" The word ripped from his throat and he plowed into her flesh like he could split her apart with his cock. "Ohhh fuck! I'm going to come!"

"Daddy! Daddy, yes!" She clung to him, her shuddering little form nothing compared to the force of him as he exploded, his cock erupting like a volcano full of white hot lava, emptying himself into the wet clench of her cunt. "Oh fuck, Daddy, my pussy feels so good! You make it so fucking good! Ahhhhh!"

Their climaxes left them gasping, breathless, him heavy on top of her, both trying to catch their breath. She blinked against the stars that floated before her eyes as she trembled with scorching aftershocks of her powerful orgasm.

"I think I won that one," she taunted him.

"You're relentless." He laughed.

"You have no idea," she challenged, seeing the light in his eyes. "But first, a woman also needs to eat!"

Naked, they ate the partially cooled steaks she'd left sitting on the stove when she'd gone to find him. After devouring their food, they went back to devouring each other. From one room to the other, in one dominating position after the other, they fucked. From the kitchen counter to the floor and back to the shower, they played a game of cat and mouse—chasing, teasing and fighting as they grabbed and kissed and bit.

Fiona even dared a few hard swats at his rock hard ass when they dried themselves again, getting into an erotic wrestling match when he grabbed her. Limbs tangled together, cock deep inside her again, they rolled over the bed to the floor, him breaking her fall, reminding her of the moment they shared back home months ago.

This time they laughed as they ascended toward that glorious, rugged apex again. Far after midnight, bodies sore and spent in the best way possible, they fell asleep wrapped in a blanket in front of the fire. By morning, she awoke to find him looking at her, a smile on his face as he lay beside her, legs still tangled, propped up on one elbow.

"You look like you got a good workout," he joked playing with her hair.

"I can only imagine the state I'm in," she said as she looked past him at the sunlight streaming in through the window. "Looks like the storm has broken."

"In some ways, yes, but in others, it's just begun," he teased.

"I'm ready for another storm," she challenged, kissing him hard.

He moved until he was on top of her, grabbing her wrists in his big hands and pinning them above her head.

"I win," he stated.

"Not until I surrender, sir," she replied as she wrapped her legs around him and moved her hips to sheath him within her folds.

"Don't call me sir," he growled, starting to fuck her again, their eyes meeting in perfect understanding and she couldn't help the smile that crept over her face. "I work for a living."

Little Brats: Georgia

The sticky juices of Georgia's wet pussy made the black, glass dildo moving in and out of her wet folds sparkle in the blue light of her laptop. The screen showed a goth guy squatting against a brick building, his black hair and pale skin making her mouth water. His fingers, draped in silver jewelry with black painted nails, gripped his not inconsiderable erection. He wore nothing other than those rings on his fingers and black combat boots. Her own hands, still dripping with heavy silver and adorned with black nail polish, were the female equivalent of his, even though hers clenched tight around the ring on the end of her toy.

"Your dick's so hard." A moan escaped her throat as she spoke to the picture on her laptop, imagining his dick as her dildo, but she was also talking, hands-free, to her cell phone sitting beside her and the guy she'd met in her college lit class who thought having phone sex would be "sick." He meant that in a good way, of course.

Nothing about him mattered other than he played a willing audience, an able participant, the masculine voice she needed to get off. He'd been willing enough when she'd offered this little date to him after class today. She snuck in the house late this afternoon still dressed in her goth attire, covered up with a jacket and hoodie. Living a double life had its positives and negatives. She loved the thrill of getting away with something, her backpack stuffed with black clothes, black spray-on hair dye, and black makeup along with all her jewelry—she changed at school each day in the library bathroom.

At home, she wore basic slacks and turtlenecks, her shoulder length hair dark, but not dark enough. The spray-on stuff made it shine a coal black. She usually returned home with her goth washed away, using the sink in that same bathroom. No one ever used it—the basement housed archives barely anyone had a need for. Yet, today, for this call, she'd pulled her hood tight and crept to her room, knowing her mother, Dorie, would be in her room nursing a migraine or nervous fit, whichever the day had brought, and her stepfather, Edward Manor—the third—would still be working at this hour.

Looking down, she admired her pussy, a pink bordering on red, glistening inside, framed by a closely cropped patch of dark curls over skin that had never seen the sun. It all struck a sharp contrast to her full, creamy thighs and the black glass toy, complete with carved head and veins. She liked it hard, and had built up a sheen of sweat pumping the thing in and out, her inner walls gripping at the thick, well-built appendage.

"Shit, I'm so hard," a male voice came from her phone, shocking her out of the fantasy brewing in her head. His voice was small, crackly, and kind of girly.

She frowned at her phone. If that continued, she knew she would have been better off just masturbating to her favorite image on the internet, making him talk dirty in her head. Seemed once this guy had his dick in his hands, his voice lost the deep timbre he'd tried to seduce her with this morning. It was his voice that had attracted her. It reminded her of someone. So did the picture on her screen—the man on her laptop looked a darker, sinister version of dominating, richly attired stepfather.

"You know, my father, he comes into my room at night, scotch on his breath, tie loosened, but still in his three-piece suit," she told the boy on the phone, letting the images in her head slip from her tongue. It was the only thing that got her really wet. "He rips back the covers, pulls up my ass, and forces his big cock into my tight hole. I tell him no. *Daddy no!* But it only makes him pound me harder. He gets what he wants, when he wants, at work or at home. He's fucked my mother into some psychotic state. Since she's close to a nervous breakdown now, he's moved onto me. At night, he finds me in these sheer, frilly nightgowns he buys me. He wants me all innocent and sweet. I fear what he'd do if he ever saw me in my black leather."

"Jesus, that's wrong!" The guy on the phone gasped and then let out a pained moan, his hand sliding up and down his cock—she could hear it, slick with some lubrication, a slap-slap-slap sound. "And so fucking hot! Tell me more!"

That encouraged her to go on, pumping the big glass cock in and out of her cunt as fast as her hand could make it go. She was getting closer. Edging toward orgasm. When she closed her eyes, she saw him, her stepfather. Fuck. The line between pain and pleasure left her winded.

Still, she went on, "I want you to come all over the tramp stamp I just got for my birthday, baby. It says *'Property of the Dark Lord'* in a gothic script. My father forbid it, but I got it anyway. My father can never see it. He never does more than lift my nightgown so he can slide into my pussy. But I want you to cover it with all your hot, dirty fucking cum."

"Oh yeah!" He groaned, his voice lower now. That was good. Very good. She could almost imagine he was her stepfather. "I want to come all over you!"

"Do it! Come for me!" She scooted her ass to the edge of her seat, spreading her legs wider, bucking up with each thrust of the glistening black cock. "Come all over my tramp stamp. Brand my ass with all that hot cum, Daddy!"

He moaned and came, shooting his load with a very satisfying growl, and Georgia arched and came along with him, seeing the goth guy on the screen holding his dick, squinting and seeing her stepfather in him, jerking his cock, coming all over her. She could almost feel the heat of the man's cum on her ass—her tattoo burned—as she shuddered and climaxed, plunging the glass cock deep into her clenching pussy.

"Oh man, that was good." The guy on the phone was an annoyance now. Georgia wrinkled her nose, reaching for her phone. "Think maybe we could—?"

As she ended the call, a movement caught her attention, her door opening a crack. She froze as her stepfather's large form appeared. Impressive in a black and gray pinstripe suit, well-groomed from head to toe, he presented a slick and menacing figure, a man everyone quickly obeyed. Including Georgia.

She should have been falling apart inside, frozen, paralyzed, humiliated, afraid to be exposed to him this way, dressed in full goth, no less, with a thick cock spreading her pussy open, but instead—her stomach fluttered. Terror seized her momentarily—but the thrill of being caught by him, what it could possibly mean, also excited her. His gaze roamed over her body, from the mess between her thighs up to her heavy breasts.

"Come to the parlor tonight." His stone-cold eyes met hers, his command meant to be obeyed. No questions. "Eleven o'clock, on the dot. Pour yourself a glass of my cognac."

With that, he was gone.

What the hell?

She looked down at herself. Not only had he caught her masturbating, but she still had her black dress bunched around her middle, hair coal black, face painted. She couldn't image what he wanted with her tonight, not after this. Surely, he wouldn't bother her frail mother with the incident. The woman's psychiatric meds didn't help her deal with the most basic elements of life, let alone something like this.

What was he going to do? What was she going to do?

She should have been scrambling to cover herself, to scrub away the evidence, but it didn't matter, not anymore. Instead, she closed her eyes, seeing him again in her mind, his gym-built body only accentuated by his well-tailored suit. She found herself torn between her fear and the excitement of being caught, hips beginning to move again. She opened her eyes, glancing down to watch the glass cock disappear inside her. Her fevered brain mixed the goth guy on the screen with her stepfather, terror with arousal, pain with pleasure, and before she knew it, her body flew again toward climax, the searing heat of her constricting muscles making her bite her lip until the metallic taste of blood graced her tongue.

Georgia walked on shaky legs to the parlor, just as instructed. Her stomach was in knots, roiled with fear, defiance, and a sick curiosity. She walked slowly, wide-eyed, trying to convince her lungs to keep working. She'd had hours to think of every possible scenario that might play out, from a father taking his daughter over his knee, humiliatingly naked, to him waiting, erection in hand, to have his way with her. Of course, none of that was likely to happen. She'd probably end up grounded, her car impounded, her phone and laptop taken away.

Even though she'd used every toy in her small arsenal to satisfy herself, her sex still throbbed as she walked now. She couldn't help it. Her fantasies were sick, but she loved them. She got herself off again and again, imagining depraved, twisted things, most of them involving her stepfather and his commanding voice, his own sick need.

She stepped inside the parlor, shoulders back, arms rigid at her sides. Standing there, she pondered the decanter of cognac and glass sitting out on the coffee table for her.

Walking slowly to the middle of the big room, one dark with rich mahogany wood and leather furniture, she picked up the decanter to pour herself a drink—she wasn't yet twenty-one, so this was an illicit act, one pre-approved by the man who'd raised her.

Her breath caught to see a glass-covered opening in the table that let her see into the room below. Her brow furrowed, realizing the heavy, wooden serving tray that usually adorned the table had been removed. She'd never been in the room below this one. It was just storage, housing expensive, unsold items for her father's auction house. That's what her mother had always told her when she ushered Georgia away from the always-locked door.

Instead of shelves of expensive items, Georgia saw her mother in a compromising position. Her body hung draped over and below three black bars on a metal table, waist high to her stepfather. Contorted and bound, body limp, Georgia guessed the woman would have slid from the table like a rag doll had she not been tied to the bars with cuffs and chains. Her arms stretched out in front of her, cuffed to the table, her head rested on them. Not one emotion showed on the woman's face. She looked strung out, in fact, maybe on her mind-altering drugs, worse than Georgia had ever seen her before. Her glassy eyes stared at nothing.

With her ass up high in the air, over the highest bar, her legs chained far apart with some sort of separator, Georgia saw a butt plug forcing the woman's ass open. Her father held a long wand in his hand, one with a round black ball on the end of that he pushed against her mother's clit, making her limp body jump and tremble. The woman began to whimper and then finally cry out, tears actually streaming from her eyes. She heard a faint grunt through the glass as her stepfather shoved this thicker-than-any-cock-she'd-ever-seen wand into her mother.

As the woman huffed and puffed, her face turning an odd shade of red, her body trying to squirm despite her restraints, her stepfather looked up at the glass opening—right at Georgia. He wore only his silver silk dress shirt, tie loosened around his neck. His erection stood out from his shirt, long and thick, veins bulging in the shaft. Pulling out the wand, he replaced it with his cock, thrusting into her up to his balls in seconds. As he forced himself in and out, he twisted the butt plug in her ass.

Georgia had seen the plugs before on the sex toy sites she frequented, but had never understood how something so large would fit in such a tiny hole. But there it was. Her mother had taken not only the plug in her ass, but now her husband's thick cock too, filling her pussy. She wasn't crying. She wasn't screaming. She wasn't really responding at all. She just laid there, inert, eyes closing, taking what he gave her. How could she not respond? Georgia wondered.

It was a strange scene—and not just because she was watching her parents having something that might be called sex—but her pussy clenched as she watched. She tried to imagine being bound that way, having something pressed into her ass and pussy at once. What would it feel like? But it looked as if her mother wasn't feeling anything. She thought the woman had to be near death not to react to all of that, good or bad.

Georgia's reaction was immediate. Her whole body filled with heat. Her pussy clenched and grew even wetter, if that was even possible. Her heart pounded, her breath turned to glass in her throat. The sight of her stepfather this way, completely in control, fucking his wife, made her want him to the point of insanity.

Her mother stared off into the distance, grimacing slightly when he pulled the butt plug from her ass. Georgia saw her stepfather now had pleasure beads in his hands. She'd seen them before online at the sex toy sites. She watched, aghast, as he pushed them one by one into her mother's puckered hole. Her own ass clenched, sending a ripple of contractions through her core. Her pussy gripped for something, anything, to invade it as roughly as he had her mother's.

A gasp escaped her as her entire body pulsed and tightened to see a tramp stamp tattooed on her mother's lower back. It was an alphanumeric code, the same used to identify items bought and sold at her father's auctions. A bar code.

No wonder he saw her as an owned object. He saw everyone that way.

Georgia heard his voice, muffled through the glass, rebuking her mother for not responding to the gifts he was giving her. He reached for something—a riding crop. Bringing the little rectangle on the end of the thin stick down on her mother's ass, the woman jumped and a red welt formed immediately. Every time he smacked her, Georgia saw his erection jump, and her insides throbbed, her breathing becoming labored. Her ass tingled. She wanted to feel the leather sting her own skin. She couldn't imagine the sensation, but oh God, she longed to experience it.

When her stepfather pulled out the beads and put a slightly bigger butt plug back in, her ass ached imagining that sensation too. Georgia's hips began to buck, her ass cheeks clenching together tight when her stepfather doled out a few more swipes of the crop over her mother's reddening ass. She was so turned on, she could barely breathe. What was wrong with her? She was watching a woman—her own mother—being tortured, and she wanted it too. She wanted to be that woman, tied, bound, things shoved into every orifice, spanked, humiliated.

Why was that so fucking hot?

Her stepfather slowly pushed a long, buzzing dildo, a piece of plastic thick and curved, into her the woman's only empty hole, pressing a button at the end of a wire hanging from her mother's folds, making the woman cry out.

Georgia fucked the air, watching her mother's hips rock and roll. She writhed in her straps. Georgia clenched her thighs together, her pussy throbbing, watching her stepfather jerking his cock as the dildo did its work on his wife. The woman was now being tortured with pleasure. Her body responded, whether she wanted it or not. Georgia's own body betrayed her too. She should have been appalled, horrified. She should have turned away in disgust.

Instead, she went to her knees so she could see better, watching her stepfather stroking his big, beautiful cock as he went around his wife's bound body, near her head. Georgia saw her mother's body jerk and convulse as her climax neared. Georgia's breath came faster and her breath fogged the glass, her pussy so hot it felt as if it was on fire. Her stepfather fed his wife his erection, making her swallow it bit by glorious bit.

"Come for me!" Her stepfather's voice boomed, his hand on the back of his wife's head as he fucked her mouth. "Come for me now!"

Georgia cried out as her stepfather looked up, straight at her. The man's wife was climaxing, shaking all over with pleasure, swallowing his cum the best she could—he spilled copious amounts of the stuff and it dribbled out the sides of her mouth—but Georgia knew, *she knew*, he was really talking to her. He wanted his stepdaughter to come. Now. Right fucking now.

And to Georgia's own shock and surprise, her body responded to his command.

She came, with such great force she thought it might tear her apart, even though *Georgia hadn't touched herself*. As the hot, quivering pulses ripped through her, stole her breath, gave her already shaking body the strength of gelation, she knelt, stunned, feeling the flood of her juices that had already soaked her panties move onto her thighs. Even as her mother shook all over with her contractions, her stepfather pulled everything from her body and unbound her.

He walked from the space Georgia could see into as her mother moved slowly, like a wounded animal, off the table to grab a robe. Her stepfather cradled the woman, soothing her, and she looked up at him with such worship and admiration, it took Georgia's breath away. She knew that feeling. She knew it well.

Georgia's phone buzzing in her pocket startled her, and she blinked a few times before she gained the wits back to grab the thing. Sliding her hand over the screen to read the text that had come through, under her father's name and number, it said, "Sitting Room. 8:00AM."

She saw him looking up at her.

Then the room went dark.

Her alarm pulled her from a deep sleep at seven-fifty in the morning. The smell of her own sex hit her first as she pushed aside her covers, littered with sex toys. Groggy, she pulled on clothes, still waking up as she ran down to the sitting room. She entered to find her father sitting on a chair, legs crossed, one arm propped up on the arm of the leather, his first two fingers swirling over his thumb.

In his weekend silk dress pants and shirt, no tie, he was a harsh contrast to her mother, the frail shell of a woman who stood in the corner, shoulders slumped, head down, in a basic black frock of a dress. Georgia entering had not even roused the woman.

"Say good-bye to your mother, Georgia." His tone was matter-of-fact. "She's traveling to Spain today to be admitted into a recovery clinic where she'll be treated and instructed to reclaim her spirit."

Her mother lifted her head slightly as Georgia went to hug the woman. Wrapping her arms around the tired, defeated skeleton, she wondered if her mother had a spirit left to reclaim. Giving her a gentle squeeze, acutely aware her mother hadn't even made an effort to raise her arms to hug her daughter back, tears stung Georgia's eyes only a second before she willed them away.

"*You* have the spirit," her mother whispered into her ear.

Pulling back, Georgia's face scrunched up in shock and horror, her mind playing through the possible implications of the woman's words as, with the ding of a bell, a servant appeared to take her mother away to a waiting car. Georgia could see it through the corner of the window.

"I expect you bathed and in the Wine Cellar Tasting Room by nine o'clock," her father demanded, his harsh tone making her jump, her ass tighten. "Wear that black whorish shit you do to school. Doll yourself up, goth-girl. And bring your toys."

She turned to look at him, willing the terror on her face into a blank stare. She'd been excited yesterday, but now, it was real. This was really happening. Fear clawed her belly. With a wave of his hand, he dismissed her. Needing nothing more than that to gratefully flee to her room, Georgia sprinted as fast as her legs would carry her through the big house to her room.

Breathing heavily, she grabbed her luggage out of her closet and began to pull her good stuff from her drawers. After tossing it in wrinkled clumps into the big suitcase, she grabbed the smaller bag and went to the bathroom to pack her secret stash of makeup and jewelry.

The man is crazy. This situation is crazy. I won't be broken like my mother by Mister Rich and Dominating. He can't have his way with me, she thought, as images from last night plowed through her head.

But that was the problem. Those images hadn't horrified her at the time. They had appealed to her. *Aroused* her. Something happened in her body, a need grew, throbbed. She wanted to see herself bound to that table. She nearly hyperventilated, imagining that butt plug in her own ass, the large vibrating wand on her clit. Her hand reached down, seeking heat, finding her cunt quivering and wet. Pushing her fingers hard against the sensation, she steadied herself.

Seeing her hairbrush on the sink, she impulsively yanked at her waistband and shoved her pants down. Grabbing the brush and cocking her hip to the side, she brought the round head of the plastic down hard on her ass. With a sharp intake of breath, she rode out the pleasure building in her body from the sting.

He'll never break me, she thought with a devious grin as she put down the brush. Kicking off her pants, she stormed half-naked to her room and ripped all the clothes back out of her suitcase. Shoving them back into the drawers, not bothering to hide them under her house clothes this time, she primed herself for what was to come.

Back in the bathroom, she literally tipped the toiletry bag so that it emptied its contents into her still open drawer. Going back to her bed, she gathered up her small collection of toys to wash off and pack up in her bag, preparing to bathe, dress, and meet her stepfather head on.

Arriving at the Wine Cellar Tasting Room a few minutes early, Georgia looked over the bottles and glassware adorning the walls and ceiling. The colors of burnt orange and desert brown were softened by strings of real dried grapevine wrapped in little white lights and plastic grapes draped over just about everything from rafters to shelves. Old wine barrels acquired at a high prices formed tables to serve and dine from.

She felt out of place in her tight black dress with lace arms, torn hose and heeled, knee-high leather boots. The top of the dress was corset-like, her breasts pressed together, pushed up high into two large, round mounds of white flesh. The heavy material of the dress clung to all of her curves, accentuating each one. She straightened her back and stood up tall, catching her reflection in the etched mirror.

Her hair, painted black and slicked into fringes around her face made a nice frame for her white powdered cheeks, heavy eye shadow and thick blue-black lipstick. She admired the way she'd painstakingly drawn wings with eye liner around her eyes, giving her full cheeks a more dramatic edge. She watched her eyes turned to slits as she heard her stepfather's footsteps enter the room.

Before she could turn to face him, he stated firmly, "First order of business is your punishment for disobeying the no tattoo rule, telling lies about me on the phone, and dressing like a devilish whore outside of this house. Second on my agenda is a reward for staying and obeying my orders. Follow me."

He turned and she obeyed, walking behind him, matching him step for step, until he stopped to unlock the door to the "storage" room. As he turned on the bright overhead lights, the table she'd seen last night loomed in the center, surrounded by a metal chest, open and filled with sex toys, along with restraints hanging from the walls and ceiling. As she scanned the wide open area, a black leather chair, ornate and throne-like, sat up on a small stage built in one corner. Crops and other punishment devices hung from a rack. The whole place was a bright, stark, white against black, and it welcomed her, made her giddy just to stand in the place.

He obviously spared no expense for his little dungeon of horrors, she thought, tightening her mouth against the devilish grin she felt threatening to break out over her face.

He slammed the door, giving her a start before he circled around her.

"You are a dramatic little deviant, aren't you?" he asked, grabbing her arm in his big hand and yanking her with him to his throne.

Sitting down, he pulled her to him, bending her over his thighs, as he laid down the law.

"You will obey my every command. You will not struggle. You will not come during your punishment."

With that, he brought his hand down twice, once on each cheek, still covered by her dress. She bit her lip to keep from crying out with the sheer pleasure, the feeling of his large hands hitting her ass. She grew wetter, his command not to orgasm giving her a moment of pause. Pulling her skirt up to expose her lace-covered cheeks, he spanked her again, just twice with his hand, one hard, resounding smack per cheek, and this time the blows were upward, causing an increased sting. The heat grew, made her want to wiggle, actually beg for more, but she clenched her ass in order to fight the urge.

"No clenching," he commanded with another set of spanks.

She felt him grab the back of her panties and pull. The lace tore, biting into her thighs as it released. She breathed through the glorious sting, her pussy trembling already. If she could come without touching herself, she feared her fate with her stepfather laying his hands on her.

"Reach your hands back and grab that gorgeous ass of yours I plan to redden every inch of," he insisted. As she moved her arms, he added, "You shall say, *yes, Daddy*, each time you obey."

"Yes, Daddy," she managed as her fingers touched her warmed ass cheeks.

Her black-painted nails cut into her flesh, and she wished she could see the sight he did. She wished she could be up above, looking down through the glass like she had before. She wanted to see herself, see him doing this to her. He hit her again, twice, making her gasp.

"Open yourself to me," he spat.

"Yes, Daddy," she said as she pulled her cheeks apart, showing him her puckered hole that tightened and released in anticipation.

"I have a fucking pain in the ass whore of a daughter, don't I?" he asked. "Look at that ass, begging me for more. Dare we find your pain threshold?"

"Yes, Daddy," she grunted out each word as his fingers hit her hole with two good taps.

She felt the tremors of the pain blissfully shoot through her core, tightening her stomach in the expectation of more.

"Spread your legs and show me that pale little pussy," he added.

She did so, feeling her inner walls pulse as she exposed herself to him. His fingers, tight together, came down with two swats on her wet folds. Her hips bucked. God, she wanted something shoved inside her. Preferably his cock.

In response, the fingers of his other hand pushed under her stomach, finding her sticky wet pussy, pressing hard against her clit. His other hand came down hard on her ass, pushing her hands aside and then falling harder than they had onto her cheeks four more times in fast clip. Each smack forced her clit harder against the pads of his fingers.

"You've already earned yourself a more severe punishment," he said, pulling her by her hair to get her to stand. He walked her over to the cuffs hanging from the ceiling and bound her hands in them up over her head. Coming around to face her, his already chiseled features held tight, he pulled at the ties on her corset-like dress. She forced herself not to wiggle against the feel of the material now laying over her stinging ass.

In strong, fluid movements, he ripped the material until she soon hung there naked, apart for her torn thigh highs and boots. He grabbed a small leather whip, a flogger with thick leather, from the wall, and without pause, brought it across her round breasts. Her nipples hardened, and she dared clench her ass and thighs against the pulsing need to be taken, invaded. Luckily he hadn't noticed as he'd moved on to whip the leather strips down along her waist, legs and back. The caress of this light torment blanketed her body—titillating torture. She was proving to be more of a pain whore than she'd even dreamed she could be.

He kicked her feet further apart as he brought the instrument of blessed misery across her red ass. The sting stole her breath, her stomach knotting, the pleasure boiling up there. She knew at this point he held back, but as he went, whipping her body, the sting grew to a glorious fire, a glow inside and out. At this point, she already wanted him so much, she would have endured anything, even if she hadn't wanted more. Each bite of pain brought her pleasure she'd never known, could never have imagined.

Reeling in her wondrous misery, punishment and lust, she opened her eyes only when he released her wrists. Moving her to the table, he boosted her up, cold and business-like, his every touch kindling the fire already smoldering within her. He arranged her over the three metal bars she'd seen her mother restrained in. The highest one was under her hips, keeping her ass high in the air. The middle one at her back, he pushed her under, and the lowest one he cuffed her wrists to. Her legs—pulled apart enough to make her muscles protest the stretch—were bound at the knees to the base of the highest bar.

"Take a minute to collect yourself while I go through your little toy collection," he said as he rubbed his hand hard over her heated ass cheek like a reminder.

"Yes, Daddy," she breathed as he went for her bag.

"This is a sad assortment." He shook his head as he pulled out her dildos, the egg and the little plastic nubby thing she wore around her finger to play with her clit.

"Yes, Daddy." She wasn't sure where he was going with this.

"Nothing for your ass either. Does that make you an ass virgin?"

"Yes, Daddy," she confessed.

"We'll do something about that," he threatened. "It may be part of your punishment the first time, but you'll learn to like it by the time you take my dick in your tight little asshole."

"Yes, Daddy." *Oh yes, yes, fuck yes.*

She watched him grab an anal plug, something a great deal smaller than she'd seen him use on her mother. Moving behind her, he brought his hand down on her puckered hole a few more times, warming it up before he dropped cold gel onto it. She couldn't help but clench, and he didn't chide her this time. Instead, he let out a low laugh, an amused chuckle.

"Relax," he said, reaching his hand between her legs, taking her own juices and smearing them over her clit.

"Yes, Daddy." She whimpered at his touch.

With the pads of his fingers, he alternated between small spanks to her clit and then circular rubs. She couldn't squirm if she'd wanted to in this position. As he continued to punish her clit, a relentless tease, he slowly eased the plug into her lubricated asshole. She felt the tight muscles resist and then finally give way. The slight burn of this invasion thrilled her pussy, made it tingle until it throbbed. With his hand still at her clit, the butt plug easing in inch by inch, she came, clenching her teeth together not to cry out, but the contractions, hard and fast, made her body tremble. She couldn't hide it from him.

"You were told not to climax during your punishment." He expressed his disapproval with a deep sigh.

"Yes, Daddy." Oh, that thing in her ass, stretching her open! It was heaven, a terrible, dark, twisted sort of torture. Her orgasm was still rocking her body, so full, so completely filled.

"Looks like you're an ass whore as well, my curvy little daughter. Still, as much as this idea pleases me, I'll have to punish you for disobeying my order with your climax."

"Yes, Daddy." She hung her head, filled with fear as well as excitement.

Before she could contemplate the meaning of this, she heard the whoosh of a riding crop through the air. The tiny bite of leather on the end hit her upper thigh first, granting her a burst of hot pain that shot to her stomach, making it flip and flutter. As he continued, the tiny implement of torture hitting her ass, the plug, even tapping from time to time against her mound, she begged him with everything, every fiber of her being, to be taken. She didn't vocalize it, but she willed it. She wanted him to take her, to fuck her harder than she ever had been before.

Her every nerve ending burned, on edge, she couldn't tell where one stream of pain began and one roll of pleasure ended. Hot, sweating, filled with lust, her stepfather pulled the butt plug out only to push it back in again. Oh fuck! That hot, burning stretch again, that tight ring of muscle. *No, Daddy, noooo!* Her mind begged him to stop, but her body pleaded that he go on and on and on.

"Your punishment for coming will be severe." His fingers moved between her thighs. He pinched her clit and she gasped. "This is mine. It belongs to me. You will never, ever come without my permission first. Understand?"

"Yes, Daddy." Her thighs trembled. Her clit pulsed between his thumb and forefinger.

"I'm going to show you that this clit belongs to me." He squeezed it and she gasped, biting her lip. "I'm going to make you climax again and again. You're bound here for my pleasure, and I can do to you what I like. You are stripped bare before me and always will be, unable to escape your own wicked desires."

"Yes, Daddy."

"Open," he said, as he arrived at her head.

She blinked to focus as he shoved, not the cock she'd been hoping for, but a ball gag into her mouth.

"My wand will make you cry out, despite your willful nature."

He disappeared back behind her again and she heard him start up the big wand he'd used on her mother. He placed the vibrating head against her clit, buzzing the poor thing to life again. She came fast and hard, in just seconds. Her vision blurred, her stomach clenched. She felt the overwhelming need to close her legs, to get a break from the pleasure, but no. This was his torture. He left the wand vibrating there.

He was right. She cried out. She begged him to stop. But words wouldn't form, not with the gag in her mouth. Multiple, forced orgasms ripped through her, tightening her stomach again and again until the muscles hurt, turning her body into a quivering mess. The aftershocks of the orgasms continued, each flowing into the next brutal rush of pleasure, until she cried out freely, seeing stars, feeling she would die from one more contraction. She screamed. She screamed as he brought her to a full orgasm again, each one harder than the last, until they blurred her vision completely.

"Good girl." He stopped the machine. Finally. That horrible, pleasure-pain buzzing had ended. "You took that well. Now, for a little reward."

Walking to the front of the table by her head, he undid his belt and pants, pushing himself out of them, revealing to her, up close and personal, his full erection. After taking out the ball gag, he did something that surprised her. He leaned in and kissed her mouth. She still wore her black lipstick, her face was wet from tears—she didn't even know she'd been crying, but she had wept through her orgasms—but he kissed her, tenderly, gently.

"You are my beautiful whore," he whispered, bent so he could meet her eyes, lifting her chin. "My deviant, twisted little daughter. You are mine. I own you, body and soul."

"Yes, Daddy," she whispered, and she meant it.

"I want to see that black lipstick smeared all over my cock." He stood, offering him her erection. "Suck it, Georgia. Suck Daddy's cock."

"Yes, Daddy," she nodded, licking her lips, opening her mouth for him as he pressed the head in. He was big, beautifully big and hard, as he thrust deep, making her gag on him.

"I want to hear you choke on it," he told her when she tried to hide her reaction. "Gag on my cock, little girl."

Georgia moaned, feeling her pussy pulse to life again as he fucked her mouth. How could she still want more? Her cunt was so swollen and hot. Almost numb from all the pleasure she'd endured. But the way he grabbed her hair and shoved himself past her teeth, deep into the recesses of her throat, set her whole body on fire.

"Take it!" He commanded, hips pumping, fucking her mouth so hard and fast she could barely breathe and didn't care. "Choke on that cock!"

Yes, Daddy. Yes, Daddy. Yes, Daddy.

She couldn't say the words, but she thought them, saliva dripping in ropes from her mouth—he was fucking her throat too fast for her to even swallow it— her eyes watering with tears. He groaned, burying himself deep in her throat, cutting off her air entirely for a moment and she panicked, gagging, trying to turn her head, but he had her hair clenched in both fists, holding her fast. Then he withdrew, rubbing the head of his cock over her lips and cheeks. Georgia gasped, seeing the remnants of her lipstick all over the shaft and head.

"You want Daddy to fuck you hard, don't you, goth girl?" He gently slapped her cheeks with his cock and her pussy clenched at his words.

"Yes, Daddy," she confessed. *More than anything, Daddy.*

"Then that shall be your reward for following my instructions. For coming here and being mine." He marked her face, a cross on her cheeks, her forehead, with the dark lipstick left over on the head of his cock. "I claim you, Georgia. Now and forever. You belong to me."

"Yes, Daddy." She trembled, her lip quivering. Tears stung her eyes, but they weren't tears of sadness. They were tears of joy, relief. "Yes. Yes. Yes."

"Yes," he repeated the word, his hand moving briefly, tenderly, through her hair. "Come when I tell you, Georgia. Come for Daddy. Yes?"

"Yes, Daddy."

He disappeared behind her. She felt the heat of his body, not touching her yet. She quivered, wanting him. She'd always wanted him, wanted this. Every moment she'd spent following his orders, acquiescing to his demands, aching to please him, wanting his love and approval, culminated here, in this moment.

She cried out when he removed the butt plug. She'd almost forgotten about it. Now she was completely empty, waiting to be filled. Now, Daddy was going to fuck her. Finally, he was going to fill her and complete her.

They both cried out when he entered her. She couldn't help it. It felt as if something monstrous had invaded her soul, something dark and thick and pulsing. Something alive and ravenous. She welcomed it, filled with pleasure beyond any she'd ever known. The thousands of little orgasms he'd forced from her with the wand was nothing compared to this. He filled her, fitting his body to hers, and then he fucked her.

Boys had fucked her before. She'd fucked herself with toys. But she'd never been fucked like this. He wasn't rough or hard on her. After the abuse she'd taken with the wand, after the spanking and the butt plug, she was tired, her muscled ached, and he seemed to know this. He rode her like a skilled man rides a just-broken horse. His cock throbbed, driving up into her, his hands gripping her hips for leverage when he came at her hard, then moving slowly over the still-stinging globes of her behind when he slowed, rolling and grinding instead of thrusting. She didn't know what would come next, couldn't see him or gauge his reactions, and she thought this was intentional.

He was in control. He knew her better than she knew herself. She moaned and cried out, she whispered her mantra, "Yes, Daddy," over and over. She remembered the way her mother had looked at the man after it was over, like she worshipped the ground he walked on, and she understood it now. Her mother had felt this, had known this secret, but she hadn't been strong enough to withstand his desire, to stand in the fire of his lust and not be consumed by it.

But Georgia could.

She let him fuck her into oblivion, her pussy clenching, gripping him, begging for more, more, more. Her body responded, even as her mind took flight. He was right. She belonged to him. She would belong to him from now until the end of time. He was no man—he was a dark god. Every movement claimed her, made her more and more his and his alone.

"Oh Daddy!" she cried as the driving thrust of his cock pushed right up to the edge. "Yes! Yes! Daddy, yes!"

"Come for me, Daughter!" he commanded, thrusting deep, grinding hard, and she did as she was told, a fierce cry escaping her throat as she came around the pulse of his cock. She came so hard, harder than she'd ever orgasmed in her entire life, body convulsing in the restraints, giving in completely, with wild abandon, to the pleasure he allowed her to take.

She moaned when she felt with withdraw, wanting to keep him in her forever.

Then he was coming too, raining white hot cum down over her ass, covering the forbidden tattoo she'd kept secret with his seed. She heard him cry out, felt the heat of his cum sliding down the crack of her ass, and heard his fierce words, claiming her once and for all.

"Now, I'm your dark lord."

"Yes, Daddy," she breathed, a smile lingering on her lips. "Yes."

Little Brats: Hanna

"Please God, forgive me for being a sinner and a whore."

Hanna woke up with the whispered words on her lips, so automatic they were unconscious. She was caught in a moment of confusion between sleep and waking, breath coming in short pants, the sensation of her fingers still moving between her thighs making her hips jerk involuntarily.

The aching flutter in her belly held the promise of her erotic dream. She made an effort to pull her sticky fingers away, but the brush of them along her wet slit swelled into a need to be filled, to be penetrated like she had been in her dream—something her mother would have dubbed a nightmare.

Hanna knew about sex. She'd read books on the subject at the library when she was supposed to be studying history or geometry, secreted away in the corner, turning pages slowly, eyes growing wider and wider as she absorbed the forbidden information like a sponge. Her panties grew wet, her sex squishy between her thighs in a way she understood, biologically—lubrication was required for the penis to enter the vagina without resistance—but confused her thoughts. She understood the mechanics perfectly. What she didn't understand was how it all made her feel.

She just knew, however she felt, she wasn't supposed to be feeling it. Her mother had guilted and shamed her from birth on the subject of sex and the woman would have been proud of herself to know that Hanna woke whispering a prayer of forgiveness for nothing more than a wet dream. A biological response, like breathing or hunger pangs.

Hanna's mind wandered, remembering her dream, even though she chided herself, told herself it was bad, wrong. She might not be in control of those thoughts when she was asleep, but she could prevent herself from thinking them when she was conscious. She worried her fingers up and down her slit like counting off beads on a rosary—although she'd never held a rosary in her life, the Catholics were all going to hell, according to her mother—her internal conflict making her hips twist. It all did nothing but serve to arouse her even more.

Her pelvis seemed to have a mind of its own, bucking and rolling, the inner walls of her vagina contracting still, as if searching for her dream man, the one who had been inside of her, pumping in and out so deliciously. What would it feel like, to have something that size deep inside her womb? Her own curiosity was torture. Her body responded, no matter what she did, her nipples growing hard, her sex wet, and it was enough to drive her mad. How was an inquisitive, inexperienced girl supposed to remain pure?

Hanna turned her flushed, red face into her pillow, remembering the man from her dream more fully, bringing her shame to the surface. Her dream man was handsome, a cowboy type, like her stepfather. Marshall Young was tall, rugged, and ripped. She'd gotten an accidental glimpse of the man's body coming out of the shower once, and it was an image she had burned in her mind. Her dream man could have been his brother, maybe even his twin, with a broad, hard chest, defined abs, a strong jaw. Her stepfather made her feel secure in his presence, and that's just how he dream man had made her feel.

Just the thought of the man who had invaded her unconscious, his flesh pressed against hers, sweaty and strong, made her skin tingle. Unable or unwilling, she wouldn't analyze now. Instead, she slipped her already wet fingers inside herself, two, then three, pushing her hips up as she forced them further in, needing to know how it felt to have something, anything, in there. Curling them, she hit a soft spot deep inside that stole her breath as she moved to the rhythm she relived from her dream, a frantic pace, as if he rode her.

She knew it was wrong. Her dream, this act, all of it was a sin. But somehow her body didn't care. Her body wanted what it wanted. It wanted this, to be penetrated, to surrender, to be pounded and ridden and taken, again and again. She plunged her fingers deeper, hearing the wet sound they made, and imagined her man's erection, thick and hard and pumping deep. Hanna longed to see his face, feel his hips bumping up against hers, his belly slick, pelvis grinding.

Oh God. Oh God, please. Forgive me, God, but it feels so good!

She knew what was coming and worked toward it. Wanted it. Shamefully, her face turned into the pillow still, Hanna bit her lip to keep herself quiet, but a little squeal still escaped her throat as the contractions began deep in her core. This was it. The moment she longed for, dreamed of, her sex contracting again and again. She rode her climax out, the man in her mind, the one thrusting deep and hard, become even more vivid. Her imagination exploded and no longer was the man just a dream, he was real, he was pounding into her with rhythmic intensity, and he was no longer unidentified.

He was Marshall Young. He was her stepfather.

Hanna cried out into her pillow, calling his name, panting as each ripple of post-orgasmic pleasure made her hips buck again, moving her fingers in deeper, increasing her orgasm, extending it, almost unbearably. She shuddered and squeezed her thighs together over the sopping mess between them, and still, the image of her stepfather emptying his seed into her eager, waiting womb wouldn't go.

She wanted it. She wanted him.

Oh God, please forgive me. I'm a sinner and a whore. I'm immoral and wanton and should be punished. Please punish me as you see fit. I am helpless to temptation. Oh God, but it's good, it's so good, so very good...

Once her body finally calmed, her hands now curled up tightly at her chest, she forced the images from her head as she began, in the aftermath, to rebuke herself for her actions and thoughts. Yet, she wondered how someone could continue to deny themselves something so wonderful. Burdened by her guilt, she couldn't find the words anymore to pray and ask for forgiveness again, so she got out of bed to clean herself up and ask her mother to help her to pray.

Clearly, she needed more help than she could get on her own.

Only, by the time she reached their room, smelling fresh from the soap she'd scrubbed herself with, her skin red from the using the hottest water she could tolerate, she stopped short at the partially open door.

Irene Young was on her belly, her hips high in the air. She wore her long, white nightgown still, so Hanna couldn't see much of her mother's body. But she could see Marshall's. He was completely nude, kneeling up behind his wife, attempting, somewhat unsuccessfully, to push his erection into her from behind.

Hanna had never seen a real erection before that wasn't an illustration in a book. It rose up, thick and long, the skin bulging with veins, reddened and practically pulsing with heat. She couldn't take her eyes off it. Her breath hitched and shuddered in her chest as he pulled back with a sigh, pumping the length in his fist before attempting to push in again. His face and chest were flushed with heat, glistening with sweat in the soft light from their small bedside lamp.

"Pastor David says that married couples should only use the missionary position," Hanna's mother protested, her hands fists, gripping the comforter. "Missionary is the only holy way."

"Fine." Marshall rolled his eyes, stroking himself again as he looked down at his wife's behind. "Turn over."

Even Hanna could tell how rigid the woman was holding her body, and now that she'd rolled onto her back, her legs were not even parted enough to allow her husband's hips through. He pushed anyway, forcing her legs wider, but she kept her thighs like a latch around him so he could barely move. Hanna watched Marshal struggle to thrust, but Irene had a vise-grip around him with her legs.

Then, her mother folded her hands and began to pray.

"Dear Lord, please make us a couple worthy of you, one who obeys your every command..."

Marshall sighed, reaching down to grab that glorious length, aiming, trying and failing to push into his wife again. Irene's nightgown hid her body completely. Like Hanna's, it buttoned all the way to the neck and brushed the floor when she walked. It was tangled around her mother's waist, mostly keeping her modesty.

"Let me see you." Marshall tugged up the edge of her nightgown, revealing the expanse of his wife's stomach. "Please. Just let me…"

"No!" She pulled her nightgown down so far, her hands pushed him away. "Don't do that! It's a sin!"

"We're husband and wife," he reminded her gently, trying to nudge his way in again, but her legs actually quivered from her effort to close them, as if she could cut him in half with her thighs alone. "Just relax a little, sweetheart. Just… let yourself go. I could… I can make you wetter with my mouth."

That did it. Hanna's mother reacted so quickly, her daughter barely had time to register what Marshall had suggested. *With his mouth? Down there? What?*

"No. Absolutely not!" Hanna's mother sat up, yanking her nightgown down. "Marshall, we need to pray."

"What do we need to pray for?" Marshall snorted, shaking his head. Hanna was fascinated by the erection in his fist. It was beginning to soften, but still.

"For your forgiveness. How could you even suggest such a vile thing?" Irene snapped. "I never should have gotten on my belly for you. It was the snake, crawling on its belly, who tempted Eve! Lord knows, I have sinned, trying to satisfy you, trying to make you happy…"

"Come on, Irene." Marshall sighed. "I just thought I might actually be able to put it inside you that way. It's not like I asked to put it in your mouth. Or your ass."

"Marshall!" Hanna's mother recoiled, grabbing a pillow and covering her body with it for extra protection.

"I'm sorry." He swallowed. "I'm sorry. I didn't mean—"

"We both need to ask God for forgiveness." Tears choked the woman's voice. "We need to ask Him to make us worthy as a couple to serve Him. Our marriage, our union, must stay pure. You know that! It is only through a pure union that we can serve Him best and reap His blessings."

"Right." Marshall watched his wife pull the covers up to her neck before she folded her hands, bowed her head, and began to pray.

Hanna watched her stepfather roll to his side, pulling the covers up on his side, covering his erection. Her mother's words were methodical, phrases learned in their church. Hanna knew most of their prayers by heart, but these words were different. She wasn't a married woman yet, so she didn't know the prayers to say for a blessed union between man and wife.

She looked longingly at Marshall, who was facing away from her—and away from his wife—his broad, strong back tanned from long hours of work in the hot sun. Hanna didn't know how her mother could resist touching him, feeling those hard planes of flesh under her hands. She knew she'd give into temptation. Irene's faith was incredibly strong—stronger than them both, Hanna thought, frowning at her mother's closed eyes and whispered prayers, her stepfather's rigid posture.

Hanna knew she wouldn't be able to talk to her mother about her dream, not now. And while she had been ready to confess her sin of masturbation, she knew she couldn't confess that either. Instead, she took a few, slow steps backward before turning on her heel to go back to her own room. She would go to sleep and pray she didn't have any more dreams.

Hanna froze when she heard her stepfather's voice. At first she thought he was yelling at her—and just hearing Marshall raise his voice was a shock, because he just didn't do that—but then she realized he was addressing his wife.

"Look at me!" Marshall snapped, his voice carrying down the hallway. "Stop that incessant muttering and look at me!"

Hanna's breath caught. She actually whimpered.

"Fine! If you're going to insist on praying for something, why don't you ask God to let me go?"

Hanna's eyes widened. Her mother murmured something but she couldn't hear it.

"You know what I mean!" Marshall's voice was still loud, strident. "I got the job in California. I could be earning twice—twice—what I'm making now! Don't you want us to have a better life? What's keeping us here, Irene? Tell me!"

Hanna's toes curled under her nightgown. California? She knew he'd been interviewing for another job, he'd been excited about the prospect. But she didn't know it was far away. The thought of leaving didn't scare her, though. She wasn't allowed to make friends at school, only church, and there weren't many people she connected with. In fact, the thought of moving, starting over—away from the church her mother insisted they attend four times a week—filled Hanna with a sudden hope.

Then her mother spoke.

"You know why." Her mother's voice rose too, although she wasn't yelling. "I told you. I prayed about it with Pastor David and he said we needed to stay."

"Because Pastor David said so?"

"Marshall, you should have heard him!" Hanna's mother cried. "He was so distraught when I told him we might move. I was one of the original members of the church, remember? He told me I'm one of his finest inspirations to stay here and do God's work. How can I leave, when he needs me? Isn't God's work more important than making more money?"

Hanna held her breath, listening.

"What if I need you, Irene?" The pain in Marshall's voice broke Hanna's heart. She longed to put her arms around him. "What about me?"

"Don't be selfish, Marshall," Hanna's mother admonished. "Let's pray. Together. Let's pray for our salvation."

Hanna sighed and headed back to bed.

She wanted to ask, but didn't know how.

Hanna stood at the counter, slicing vegetables for stew beside her mother, wondering just how to approach the subject. Well, subjects, plural. There was God. That was a subject her mother was well-versed on. But Hanna wanted to add boys, or men, to that equation. The problem was, she didn't know how it added up. And when you threw sex into the mix, things got even more confusing. It turned into an impossible problem she couldn't easily solve.

She glanced at her mother. Her head was bent, focused on chopping carrots, but her lips moved silently. She was whispering prayers, even now. Her mother seemed to have all of the answers. She knew how God wanted them to live, often beginning her answers with "Pastor David says…" The woman worshipped the ground he walked on, as if he himself were the messiah come back to life. The problem was, Pastor David's view of the world—and the Bible—was very narrow.

"Mom…" Hanna took a deep breath, trying to bolster her courage, as she sliced up the last of the potatoes. "What does God want of an unmarried woman before she finds a husband? What is she supposed to do when she feels… attracted… to a man?"

"Well…" Her mother paused in her abuse of the carrot in her hand. She had worked up a sweat peeling them, as if the poor things had wronged her. "Pastor David says women mustn't give into the temptation of the pleasures of the flesh. Pastor David says, even once a couple is married, sex is only for reproducing—and, on occasion, to keep a husband faithful and away from loose women who would throw themselves at them. Or…

"Or?"

"Or from…" Hanna's mother blinked and pursed her lips for a moment before giving a small, delicate shudder. "From abusing themselves."

Hanna thought she knew what this meant, at least in theory—the book she'd read had covered topics like masturbation—but she wasn't going to ask her mother for specifics.

"How will I know when I meet the right man? What would God have him be like?" Hanna asked as she carefully placed handfuls of potatoes in the big stew pot.

"Well, you need to look for a godly man," her mother began. "Pastor David gave the best talk at our bible study on being a Godly couple. He said a couple needs to follow how love is described in the Bible in 1 Corinthians 13. A man must be patient and kind, as it says love is."

"Like Marshall?" Hanna had always believed her stepfather to be both of those things—until last night, anyway.

His angry words had echoed through her head as she rolled around in her bed, trying to get to sleep. She'd thought of them again as the sun came up and her alarm went off. She couldn't imagine her life without Marshall. He was the only father she'd ever known—her biological dad had died when she was very young, too little to even remember him—and the thought of losing Marshall, too, brought a lump to her throat.

"Yes, like my Marshall. He does his best to be Godly." Her mother sounded so pious, like she was talking about her naughty little boy who tried hard to be good. It was demeaning, even angering to Hanna. Did her mother really believe Marshall was a bad or unholy man? "He does his best to protect us, and he's not proud or boastful, not easily angered. You'd be very fortunate to find a man like him."

Did her mother feel fortunate, though? She clearly wasn't showing Marshall that she felt fortunate. Aside from whatever was happening in the bedroom—and that was none of Hanna's business—every other phrase out of Hanna's mother's mouth was about Pastor David. And wasn't a wife supposed to follow her husband? If Marshall had a job opportunity in California, why was her mother following Pastor

David's advice, rather than supporting her husband? It didn't make sense.

Hanna dog-eared the Christian novel her mother had loaned her—Irene told her daughter she should read it for inspiration to act like a proper Christian woman—and put it aside on her bed. Something had disturbed her, besides the protagonist in her book, who talked about God's will almost as much as her mother—a noise. A low sound. The wind moaning outside?

She was supposed to be at church with her mother at women's bible study, but Hanna had begged off, saying she was having her "woman time." It wasn't true, but she just couldn't face Pastor David's smug, smiling face. Not today. Her belly was still in a turmoil over her dilemma, and her mind hadn't caught up with her feelings, after everything she'd seen between Marshall and her mother.

Marshall had come home from work—she'd heard him come up the stairs. Usually, she would have called out to him, asked how his day was, but she hadn't. She was still too ashamed of what she'd seen. She could get the image of him out of her mind, his erection in his hand, the look of lust on his face.

Hanna sat up in bed, listening. The sound came again, louder this time. A low moan. Was Marshall ill? She stood, cocking her head, hearing another muffled moan through the walls. Poor man. He worked so hard. His job as a physical therapist was time consuming, and when he wasn't working, he spent as much time as he could riding horses. He liked to take Hanna riding with him on the weekends. Irene hated horses and refused to go.

Hanna had been surprised to hear him home so early. He usually went riding while they were at women's bible study. But this explained it. He'd come home sick, thinking his wife and daughter at church, when Hanna was here the whole time.

She went to his door, hesitating a moment before she knocked.

No one answered. A groan swallowed the light rap of her knuckles on the door, a throaty sound of pure misery. The door wasn't fully closed and her knock had opened it just a crack. She could see him sitting on the edge of the bed, flannel shirt still on but open, revealing his broad chest, jeans pulled down around the tops of his cowboy boots, the ones her mother forbid him to wear into the house.

Marshall had his erection gripped tightly in his fist.

She knew instantly what he was doing. It seemed to Hanna he was determined to break every rule he could, his wife's and God's. She also knew she should turn around and go back to her room and pray. Pray a lot. But she didn't. In the conflict between sin and curiosity, curiosity won out. She watched him abuse himself, fascinated by the shameful, sinful act her stepfather was committing. She had, after all, done it to herself. She knew how good it felt, how tempting it was.

The muscles in Marshall's strong thighs tightened as his hips bucked up off the bed—just like hers had last night. His hand, slick with some sort of substance the made the tight skin of his male parts all shiny, moved up and down, squeezing up over the bulbous head and then moving down to the wondrous sack that hung between his thighs, cupping them, big and heavy.

He panted, eyes screwed shut. From all appearances, he seemed to be torturing himself. No wonder her mother had called it abuse. The faster his hand moved, the louder his groans, the redder the skin along the shaft. The veins there bulged. His moans became growls deep in his throat, his ridged stomach tightening, accentuating each muscle. Between her own thighs, she felt dampness, a soft dew, the telltale sign of sin.

His movements grew more frantic, fist rising up and down his manhood, his face scrunched up as if he was in pain. He let out a primal cry, like and animal, as he grabbed himself and squeezed. Hanna saw a slow spill of clear liquid from the head of his erection, dribbling down over his fingers. He was squeezing it so hard his fingers were practically purple and he gave another cry, this time, murmuring, "Fuck! Not yet! Not yet!"

Hanna had never heard Marshall swear before.

She gasped, pulling her own thighs tighter together, that soft squish between them drawing a soft moan from her throat. She didn't mean to make a sound, didn't even register she had, until Marshall opened his eyes and looked right at her.

"Hanna." His voice was hoarse, pained.

He reacted quickly, pulling the afghan always folded nicely at the bottom of the bed, the one her mother herself had crocheted, into his lap to cover his erection.

"I'm sorry." Hanna blinked, her voice barely a whisper. "I didn't mean. I thought you were…"

"It's okay." He attempted a smile and for a minute, he was the Marshall she knew. "Come in, sweetheart.

She hesitated, a little afraid, but she opened the door enough to step just over the threshold. He was covered now, after all. And... she had questions. Maybe, if her mother couldn't answer them, Marshall could?

"Mom says..." Her hand still gripped the doorknob so tight her knuckles were white. "Mom says Pastor David says what you're doing is a sin. It's not godly. Just today, Mom said that men... do this. They abuse themselves this way. But..."

"But...?" Marshall urged her to continue.

"Sometimes I..." She bit her lip, her cheeks flushing with heat. "I feel things. Sometimes I... abuse myself too."

"Oh Hanna." Marshall frowned, a pained look crossing his face. "It isn't self-abuse. It's self-pleasure."

"Self-pleasure." She tried the words out in her mouth. That felt better than calling it abuse. But wasn't it a sin?

"Pleasure is a gift from God," Marshall said, shaking his head, looking sad. "Why would he make it pleasurable, if He didn't want us to enjoy it?"

"I don't know." She swallowed, trying to think of what Pastor David would say. *He'd tell you to turn around and go to your room and pray for forgiveness, that's what he'd say.* But she didn't do that. "Maybe... maybe it's Satan's way of tempting us?"

"No, Hanna." Marshall smiled. "God intended a man and woman to find pleasure together, through each other's bodies. That's why he designed us the way he did, to fit together."

"But you weren't... with a woman... just now..." Hanna swallowed, remembering him pleasuring himself, the sounds he made, the look on his face. She couldn't help picturing his erection, knowing it was there, just under the blanket. "If it isn't to make a baby, isn't it a sin?"

"Our bodies were made for pleasure." He met her eyes and there was a heat in them that made her feel warm all the way to her toes. "Pleasure puts us in touch with God. And nothing feels better than sex, Hanna. It's the closest we can come to feeling the unexplainable bliss that waits for us in Heaven."

"Even if you're pleasuring yourself?"

"Yes." He nodded slowly. "Sex is a biological need. Like hunger. It needs to be sated. God wants us to feel that pleasure, whether we're alone or with a partner."

"So... it's not wrong?" Hanna swallowed past her shameful question and managed to get it out. "It's not wrong for a woman to pleasure herself? To think about... men? Naked... men?"

"No, sweetheart." His voice was soft, gentle. "You're not wrong."

The relief that flooded her was incredible.

"You touch yourself?" he asked, cocking his head at her. It seemed to surprise him.

She nodded, biting her lip.

"And you think about men naked?" This seemed to surprise him even more.

"Sometimes," she confessed. "Mostly I dream about them. In my dreams, he's tall and handsome. Like you. He's... he has a big... erection..."

Had she really just said that word out loud?

"Like you..." her breath was coming in little gaspy gulps. "And he puts it inside me. I wake up shivering all over. Sometimes I put my fingers inside, just so I can feel what it might be like…"

"But you've never had sex?"

"No!" She stared at him, aghast. "I'm a virgin! And sometimes I touch myself, it's true, but Daddy, I always beg God for forgiveness afterwards."

She stated this last in a flurry of words as her hands came to an automatic prayer position at her chest.

"You don't need to ask God to forgive you, baby." He shook his head, looking sad. "God loves you and He wants you to feel loved. Sex is part of that. It's an expression of love."

"Even when I do it to myself?"

"Don't you love yourself?"

Hanna giggled.

"Come here." He held his hand out to her.

Hanna forced her feet to move toward him, unlocking the fingers laced together over her chest as she approached, her breath shallow in her throat. He slipped his warm hand into hers, pulling her to the bed to sit beside him.

"Are you afraid of me?" His thumb moved over her hand, stroking gently.

"No, Daddy." She lifted her gaze to meet his eyes.

"Who was the man in your dream, Hanna?" he asked softly.

She stiffened at his words. Oh, she didn't want to confess this. It was too much.

"I… don't know." She swallowed, shaking her head. "It was just a dream."

"Sometimes our dreams tell us what we really want."

"They do?" She couldn't help but remember her dream man now, with him so close. It had been Marshall she was dreaming of. She was sure of it.

"Was it a boy you know?"

She nodded, feeling her cheeks flush, her breath catch.

"Who was it, Hanna?" His eyes searched hers. "Who did you imagine was making love to you?"

"I can't." She heard her throat click as she swallowed, avoiding his eyes. But her stepfather took her chin in hand, tilting it so she had to look at him.

"Tell me."

"It was…" Her chin quivered in his fingers. She barely got the words out, in a choked whisper. "Oh Daddy… it was you."

"Sweet girl." He leaned in and kissed her.

His lips were soft, warm. It was sweet at first. Chaste. A tender, gentle kiss. Fatherly.

And then, his mouth moved, slanting. His tongue sought entrance. Hanna moaned and opened to him as his hand moved behind her neck, keeping her pulled in tight. She barely registered what was happening. This was her stepfather she was kissing! Her mind railed. But her body responded. Her sex throbbed. Her nipples hardened under her blouse. Her back arched as she tried to get herself as close to him as she possibly could.

This was her stepfather, but it was also her dream man.

"Oh Daddy, I'm sorry." Hanna felt tears prick her eyes as they parted. "I never should have told you. I didn't mean to. I just… wanted you so much. In my dream, I mean. I wanted… ohhhh, I wanted it."

"If you love a man, it's not wrong to want him," her stepfather whispered. His gaze was on her mouth and his thumb moved there, rubbing her lips.

She thought that over. She did love him, after all.

"I know your mother tells you it's a sin." He swallowed, his gaze moving down to her blouse, buttoned up tight, but her nipples showed, hard points, even through both blouse and bra. She couldn't help arching a little, straining those little nubs against the fabric. The sensation made her feel dizzy and faint. "She'll never teach you what it should be like, between a man and a woman."

"Will you teach me?" she asked quickly, biting her lip. "Teach me what it's like?"

"Hanna…" He took a deep breath. "I think—"

"Show me," she urged him. "Show me, Daddy. Please?"

He let a hand move through her soft, long blonde hair.

"You want me to show you?"

She nodded, eager.

"You want to learn how a man and a woman join together?" he murmured the question. "About what they can do for each other to bring us as close to Heavenly bliss as we can get on earth?"

"Oh yes," she breathed. He made it sound even better than she imagined.

"Sometimes I can't believe my daughter's a woman now, old enough to marry." He smiled, his fingertips brushing her cheek. "It makes me sad to think that your mother has already poisoned your mind against it. I don't want that to ruin your marriage, your chance for happiness."

"Then show me, Daddy." Hanna squirmed on the bed. "I love you. You said it wasn't a sin, if you loved someone…"

"And I love you." He met her eyes when he said the words. "I suppose I'm the best one to teach you."

"You are," she agreed. "I know it."

Her dream had been a sign, she was sure of it, pointing to this moment.

"You've probably only seen a penis in health or biology books, right?" he asked, smiling when she nodded. "Let me show you what it looks like."

Her stepfather tossed the afghan to the floor and she gasped to see his erection standing up tall, rock hard.

"Don't be afraid." He smiled at her wide eyed look. "It goes by many names, although the common slang is usually cock or dick."

"Cock." She tried the word out as she looked as his throbbing member. Cock. She repeated it in her head. Just thinking the word made her feel warm. So she tried out another. "Dick."

"Good girl." He praised her, his erection—his *cock*—bobbing gently in response.

"When a man gets aroused, it gets hard, like this." He glanced down at his lap and so did she. "Blood pumps into it, making it grow. Here, give me your hand so you can feel how hard the shaft is and how spongy the head."

He took her fingers, running the pads of them over his flesh. Her breath came faster as she touched the veined shaft, amazed at how soft the skin was, how it moved. The head was spongy, just like he said, and the tip glistened. Her fingers were sticky with the stuff.

"You can squeeze it," he assured her. "It doesn't hurt."

Hanna wrapped her little fist around the length of him and squeezed. Her stepfather let out a long, low moan.

"You said it didn't hurt." Hanna withdrew her hand in surprise.

"It doesn't." He took a deep breath. "It feels good. That was the sound of pleasure."

"Ohh." She reached for him, squeezing again, hearing him groan in response. "That was the noise you were making earlier."

"Yes." He nodded agreement.

"But your hand was moving." Hanna mimicked his earlier motion, up and down, feeling his hips move with her, that low sound escaping his throat again. "Like this."

"Yes," he panted. "Oh that's good. Sweetheart, your hand feels so good on Daddy's cock."

"It makes me feel good too." She met his eyes, her breath coming faster. "Down there."

"That's good." He smiled. "That's normal. You know how it works, don't you?"

"I read a book," she confessed. "In the library. I know about vaginas and penises, about the sperm and the ovum. All that stuff."

"Not very sexy, is it?" he laughed.

"No," she admitted, although she had found it intriguing. "But this is."

"So you know what these are?" He slid a hand down to cup the heavy sack between his legs.

"Testicles. They hold the semen."

"Right. They go by many names too, but usually they're called balls." He smiled. "They're very sensitive. You have to be careful with these."

"Okay." She watched, fascinated, as he took her hand and moved it down to cup his testicles. His *balls*. Oh that word made her feel funny.

"You can massage them gently." He showed her, pressing a hand over hers. "I like to have mine cradled and squeezed, lightly. Just a little, like this. Mmmm. I also like to have them sucked on."

"Sucked on!" She gaped at him.

"Yes." His eyes danced as he looked at her shocked expression. "My cock too."

That didn't make any sense to her at all. Penises in vaginas made perfect sense. That was how you made babies. But what purpose did putting his cock—or his balls—in her mouth serve?

"It feels good," he reminded her, as if he was reading her mind. "It's about pleasure. The more pleasure we can give each other, the closer we'll get to God."

"Really?" She cocked her head in wonder, squeezing his balls gently in her hand, hearing his breath become more ragged as she explored. His hips began moving, his moans growing louder, and she pulled her hand back, alarmed. "Is it okay? Was I hurting you?"

"No, sweetheart," he assured her, guiding her hand back between his legs. "You can touch me anywhere you like. Here, let's make this easier."

"We won't tell your mother about my boots or this little lesson, right?" He pulled off his boots, grinning as she watched. "It'll be our secret."

"Okay," Hanna readily agreed.

"She'd think it wrong." Her stepfather slipped out of his jeans and boxers. "But she's the one who's so horribly wrong."

"That's because she lets Pastor David think for her, instead of thinking for herself." The words escaped Hanna's mouth and she clapped her hands over it quickly, but that barn door had been opened, the horses already released.

"It's true." Her stepfather laughed. "Smart girl. Come here."

Hanna let him take her by the upper arms, gently guiding her down to kneel between his open thighs.

"I'm going to show you how to take a man into your mouth." His hand moved in her hair. "How to suck on him to make him as big as he can be, so he can pleasure you."

"Oh I like that idea."

"Me too." He chuckled. "Are you afraid of it?"

She shook her head, gazing at his cock. "I think it's beautiful."

"Do you?" he smiled. "Go ahead and touch it. Like you were before."

Hanna grasped it in her fist, liking the way it made him moan when she began to stroke it up and down, like she'd seen him do. She liked the way it pleased him.

"Would you like to try putting it in your mouth?"

She nodded, leaning in, eager, but his hand in her hair kept her at bay.

"Easy," he urged. "No teeth. That could hurt. Just your lips and your tongue. Round those pretty lips over your teeth and take as much of it into your mouth as you can."

He moved her head to him until the head of his cock rested against her lips. She couldn't breath as her heart thumped in her chest like a rabbit's foot. As he lifted his hips, sliding himself into her mouth, she curled her lips as he'd said. She didn't want to hurt him.

"Now, lick it. Roll your tongue around it. Feel the veins. Get it wet. Move your fingers through the wetness until you can easily slide them up and down. This makes him hard for you." His last sentence ended with a hiss of air over his teeth as she obeyed.

His penis—his *cock*—was swollen, engorged, filled with blood, throbbing under her tongue. His skin was salty and she licked the head, curious about that sticky liquid. That tasted peppery, almost hot, like it might burn her tongue. Salt and pepper. That's what cock tasted like. The realization excited her. Hanna knelt up, squeezing him in her fist as she leaned in, taking more of him into her mouth. It was a little scary—he was big—and she could only take about half of it before she withdrew with a gasp.

"Very good, for a first try." He smiled down at her, hand moving through her hair. "Ready to try again?"

"It feels good?" she tipped her head back to meet his eyes.

"Oh yes, very good," he assured her, guiding her head back between his thighs.

Hanna let him, aiming his cock, taking it into her mouth, further this time, slightly more than halfway. But this time she didn't pull away. This time she moved him deeper into her throat, feeling the pressure of his hand on the back of her head, urging her on. The rhythm was easy, up and down, although the faster she went, the dizzier she felt. Still, she persisted. She liked the way it made her feel—the motion made her sex ache with need. She also liked the way it made him feel. His soft cries and low moans made her tremble with lust.

She knew she should feel guilty, but for some reason, she didn't. In fact, that nagging weight of shame she carried with her always, like an elephant sitting on her chest, began to lighten until it fell away completely, nearly forgotten. Being with Marshall had the exact opposite affect she imagined it would.

"Oh fuck, sweetheart," he moaned as he grabbed her hair, not hard, using it to move deeper, his hips rising. When the tip hit the back of her throat, she gagged and pulled back, eyes watering as she blinked up at him in surprise, more because of the profanity than his enthusiasm.

"It's okay." He smiled, looking sheepish. "Sorry. It felt so good I got a little carried away. It's been a long time since... well... it's quite a gift to have a woman's mouth around your cock."

"You... swore..." Hanna tried to catch her breath. She'd never heard foul language come out of his mouth before. Ever.

"Words only have the meanings we place on them." He smiled, petting her hair. "Aside from taking the Lord's name in vain, how do we know a word is profane? Have you seen a list of forbidden words written in the Bible?"

She shook her head.

"We've decided the word 'fuck' is profane, but why?" He shook his head. "They're just words. Erection, dick, cock, breasts, pussy... they're just words. And they're actually very useful words."

"Useful... how?" Hanna swallowed, hearing that string of words coming from her stepfather's mouth making her feel tingly all over.

"It's the language of lovers," he explained. "We can use those words to tell each other what we like, to increase our pleasure."

"Ohhh." She nodded her understanding, her gaze falling to his erection. It was still wet from her mouth, and it hadn't waned in the least while they'd been talking. In fact, it seemed even bigger to her, more swollen, and a bit of clear liquid appeared at the tip.

"Look what you did." He smiled, rubbing his thumb over the head, spreading the fluid.

"Is it bad?" Hanna frowned.

"No." He chuckled. "It's good. Very good. That's a little bit of pre-cum. It means you made me very, very excited."

"I thought I tasted it, before." She swallowed, feeling hungry as she looked at his swollen length. "Kind of... peppery. Hot."

"Did you like it?" he asked, touching her cheek, the backs of his fingers brushing her skin.

"Yes." She leaned in, eager, licking the drop of pre-cum off the head of his cock. Marshall moaned softly when she did that, watching her pink tongue snake around and around. But he wouldn't let her suck him again. Instead, he reached down to lift his heavy sack, rolling his balls in his hand.

"Would you lick to try licking these?" he offered and Hanna leaned in, eager to please him. "Gently. Get them wet with your tongue first... mmm yes, like that... now suck one into your mouth... ohhhh yes... such a good girl..."

Hanna preened under his praise, exploring him with her tongue. They were heavy, but pliable, nothing at all like the hard length of his cock bobbing over her head. She sucked at one, gently, remembering his admonition, then the other, amazed and amused at the way they moved in her mouth. His cock wept clear fluid in response and she reached for it, fascinated, slowly stroking him as she licked and sucked his balls.

"Ohhhh wait, wait," he gasped, pulling back, but not before Hanna felt his thigh trembling against her cheek.

"Did I do it wrong?" She was afraid to disappoint him, especially since he was being so generous with her, sharing his body and his wisdom.

"No, no," he reassured her, pulling her to her feet. "Quite the opposite. You were so good with your mouth, you almost made me come."

"Oh." She brightened at this thought.

"But I want to be inside you," he reminded her, making her tremble at the thought. "I want to show you what it's like, what pleasure we can have together. A man can bring a woman great pleasure, and not just with his cock. He can use his hands and mouth too, like you did with me."

Hanna's eyes widened, but she didn't say anything. His hands or mouth on her seemed unfathomable, though she knew about it from biology and books.

"Undress for me," he said.

She stood there a second, her body swaying at the thought of being naked in front of him. Her mother had cautioned her since she was young to cover herself fully except when bathing. Even in the bath, she was told to always use a cloth, to never let her fingers touch her breasts or between her legs as she had just done last night.

"Don't be shy." His gaze moved over her body, still clothed, and that made her feel warm.

But her shaking hands remained poised over the buttons dotting the front of her neck-to-floor calico dress—her mother made them, sewing lace at the collar, the hem, and at the cuffs of the long sleeves—so he reached up to undo the buttons for her. She stood there, arms down now at her sides, letting him undress her, moving her like a doll as he stripped her, not only her dress, but her white cotton bra and panties and socks as well.

She fought the urge to cover herself as his hungry eyes roamed.

"You're so beautiful, Hanna." His hands settled at the curve of her waist, his eyes meeting hers. "Never hide this body from a man you love. You have curves in all of the right places. Part of what arouses a man is seeing a woman like this, touching her body."

"It arouses... him?" She crinkled her nose in confusion, biting her lip when he placed his hands on her breasts, shivering when his thumbs brushed her nipples. "But..."

"But it arouses you too?" He nodded, watching her face as he pressed her nipples with his thumbs, making her moan.

"Yes," she whispered. "When I touch myself... oh, it feels so good, Daddy. She told me it was wrong, and I felt so guilty but..."

"It's not wrong to feel pleasure." His hands kneaded her breasts. "And you should fulfill those urges when you don't have a husband to do it for you."

"It's really okay?" she frowned at this conflictual information, but the way he rolled her nipples, sending hot, tingly sensations between her thighs, distracted her.

"It's more than okay," he reassured her. "It's good. Even when you have a husband, you should pleasure yourself if you want to."

"Really?" It was all so confusing. "But I thought, once I was married, that he would be the one who…"

"Oh of course, he will." Marshall's hands moved down her body, over her soft curves. "I'm going to show you everything a man should do for you, so that once you're married, you won't be afraid and you can give yourself fully to him."

Her nipples were achingly hard. The skin tingled as it tightened. She felt a rush all the way down between her legs where she had already grown wetter.

"Your nipples are beautiful." Marshall eyed them like a kid in a candy store. "Someday they'll feed a baby, but right now they're just for pleasure. I'm going to show you how your nipples get even harder, like my erection, when they're sucked on."

When his full, wet and warm lips formed around one, gave it a small suck before flicking the tiny nub with his tongue, she groaned, her knees going weak. Between her thighs, way up inside her, she pulsed like she had after her dream the other night, a feeling that created an undeniable urge to have something inside her.

"Oh Daddy," she whispered, her hands in his hair, head going back as he moved to her other nipple, sucking so long and hard, her stomach tightened into a hard ball before it released and something like nervous butterflies fluttered through her middle.

"Does that make your pussy wet?" he whispered, flicking her nipple with her tongue.

She nodded, flushing at that word. *My pussy.* It sounded so foreign and strange, but exciting too.

"Come here." He guided her, pressing her onto the bed. "On your back. Good girl. Now... let your legs fall open."

She looked up at him, biting her lip, too afraid to show him so, with gentle hands, he pushed her knees apart.

"Oh Hanna," he breathed, eyes glassy as he stared between her legs. "You're pussy is so beautiful. So... fucking... beautiful..."

He throat clicked as he swallowed.

"You like it?" She blinked in surprise at his reaction.

"Have you ever seen yourself?" His gaze lifted and he met her eyes. "Have you ever seen how beautiful you are down there?"

"No!" She gasped at the thought. She couldn't remember looking down there at all, not since long before she started growing sparse, blonde hair in her nether regions.

"I can *see* how wet you are..." Her stepfather's gaze moved again between her thighs. "Look, let me show you."

He moved to take a hand mirror from her mother's dresser, one that had been passed down, mother to daughter. It was an old, antique thing with a long gold handle. Her stepfather gave it to her, positioning it so Hanna could lift her head, look down, and see. The curly blonde hair between her legs covered her swollen, glistening wet folds, but she could see how pink her flesh was.

"Isn't it beautiful?" he murmured and Hanna nodded, not trusting her voice.

She kept hearing her mother's voice and fought those feelings. She was supposed to feel guilty about being naked in front of her stepfather, to be doing such things with him, such wonderful things. Her mother didn't believe in too much pleasure. In fact, *Pastor David said*—always that phrase, uttered from her mother's mouth—pleasure should be used as a gauge to stop people from sinning. If it felt good, you knew it was wrong.

Only, this felt so right.

Marshall finally removed his shirt before he got on the bed on all fours between her wide open legs. Her whole body tingled just having him so close. Then, instead of taking her, entering her like she expected him to and was braced for, he settled himself between her open thighs. Hanna looked down at him in surprise and wonder as he held the mirror, angled so she could see.

"See this here?" His finger moved over a tiny nub at the top of her cleft, that secret spot, the one that, when touched, thrilled her like nothing else ever had. Her bottom clenched tight at his touch and she gasped out loud. "This is your clitoris. Is feels good to be touched here, doesn't it? Do you like that?"

"Ohh yes," she breathed.

"You've rubbed this spot before?" He passed his finger over that spot, back and forth, and she cried out. Her body felt tight, strung taut, like he was plucking a guitar string, making her whole being sing. "Until you climaxed?"

"Yes," she confessed with a little nod of her head.

"But you've never had it kissed or licked?"

"No!" Hanna watched in the mirror as he rubbed it with his fingers, rubbing her wetness over the hood of her clit.

"Does that shock you?" he smiled, kissing the inside of her thigh. His breath was warm, his lips soft. "I love to kiss and lick a woman there. I love the taste, the way she feels in my mouth. Can I kiss you there, Hanna?"

"You really like it?" She frowned, disbelieving, but nodded her assent when he reassured her with a groan and a fervent nod of his own.

Then his mouth moved between her legs, his tongue darting out to part her folds, moving back and forth until it nestled itself at the top of her slit. Her fingers—and his—felt incredible. But this? This was bliss. Pure heaven. This must be what angels felt every minute of the day. All of her denied desires broke through whatever was left of the wall her mother had built, flowing out of her like honey.

"Oh Daddy!" she moaned, her hips rocking up to meet his flickering tongue. "Oh that feels so... so... ohhhhh!"

"Mmm," he agreed, fastening his mouth over her mound, sucking and licking, the heat of his tongue lashing her again and again.

Hanna grabbed the mirror from him, angling it so she could watch her stepfather lick her wet pussy. She marveled at it, not just the sensation, but watching his tongue flick and tease her clit, sucking at that little bit of flesh, his breath hot. One hand held the mirror, the other moved in his hair, her hips moving all on their own, pressing up, wanting more, more, more, until it was difficult for him to follow her and he grabbed her ass in his big hands.

"Oh, I'm sorry," Hanna apologized, shame flooding her cheeks. "Am I supposed to keep still?"

"No, sweetheart." He chuckled. "That's a natural movement. You'll move just like that when I'm inside you. But I want to make you climax like this first. You taste so good. Look how wet and delicious you are."

She was looking. The mirror reflected the way his tongue flattened, moving between her lips, brushing downward over her hole. That's where he would slide inside of her, she knew. His tongue probed there, sucking and licking her juices, before slipping upward again. When he reached the very top, she moaned, pushing up again with her hips.

"Oh Daddy, yes, right there," she moaned, dropping the mirror so she could run both hands through his hair. "Please! Please!

She found herself begging him again and again, her body trembling on the precipice of that hot rush of contractions she'd experienced the night before at her own hand—only this was stronger. So much stronger. The sensation of his wet tongue was something sublime, beyond anything she'd ever experienced. He didn't let up, flicking his tongue and sucking in a glorious rhythm. Her hips moved, faster, the wet sound of his face buried between her legs filling the room.

"Oh! Daddy! Oh now, please, now!"

He grunted and grabbed her behind in his hands, squeezing and pulling her close as her orgasm overtook her. The tremors shook her heated body, muscles tightening and releasing, her toes curling as she quaked in his arms, thrashing on the bed. The sensation filled her with a bright, shuddering light, a fire that blurred all sensation into a pinnacle of sheer bliss that she feared, for a moment, might actually drive her mad.

She opened her eyes when he laid his body over hers. She welcomed him, his chest heavy, his erection nestled between their bellies, as he pressed his wet lips to hers.

"Taste yourself," he murmured as he swept his tongue to part her lips.

The musky, sweet taste of her own wetness lingered in her mouth as she kissed him back. She'd kissed Marshall a million times, light pecks goodnight, but this was something else altogether. His mouth was full of secrets, his tongue seeking entrance, just like his cock throbbing against her navel. He wanted inside of her, to devour and consume her. And she wanted it too.

"Please," she whispered when they parted. "Put it inside me. I want to feel you."

He nodded, drawing a shaky breath.

"It may hurt you," he warned softly, reaching down between them to cup her mound. It was still wet and swollen from her climax and she moaned softly. "Have you ever put anything inside you before?"

"No." She shook her head.

"Not even your fingers?" His probed her as he slid one long finger into her hole.

"Well yes…" she flushed. "My fingers sometimes."

"Anything else?" he inquired. Two fingers now. Hanna shivered and moaned as he rocked his hand, moving them, in and out. "A sex toy?"

"No!" Her eyes widened. "Never!"

"I'll teach you about toys some other time." He smiled. "Your mother thinks they're tools of the devil, but they're not. Nothing else? A candle? A carrot? A cucumber? Girls get curious sometimes…"

"No." Hanna shook her head vehemently, although now that he mentioned all of those things, her mind exploded with the possibilities.

"So it really will be your first time." He nodded, slipping a third finger into her. She gasped and squirmed. "I promise, I'll go slow. If it hurts, you tell me. There may be a moment of pain when I break your hymen."

"I read about that," she offered, her body tensing, not knowing what to expect.

"It's only once," he soothed, his fingers moving slowly in and out of her wetness. "Do you trust Daddy?"

She nodded, meeting his eyes, but she felt her bottom clench at the thought.

"Shhhh, sweetheart." He kissed her cheek, shaking his head. "Relax. Don't tense up. It will only make things more difficult."

Hanna nodded, taking a deep breath. She remembered him saying that to her mother, how the woman and tried to close her legs, even as he tried to enter her. She didn't want to do that. She wanted to please him.

"Easy, I'm just going to rub the head of my cock against your pussy, okay?" His fingers were gone from inside of her, but then there was another sensation, a fat, spongy head sliding through her slit, up and down. Hanna moaned when it rubbed up against her clit, biting her lip when he neared her virgin hole.

"Doesn't that feel good?" he breathed. "I won't do anything without telling you, I promise. Okay?"

"Okay," she breathed, putting her arms around his neck. "I'm ready. I am."

"Good girl." He kissed her softly, his tongue probing, mimicking that same motion between her legs. His cock was aimed right at her hole. "Okay, sweetheart, Daddy's going to put his cock inside of you now."

"Yes." She swallowed, taking a deep, shuddering breath before letting her knees fall open further. This was it. This was really it. He was going to take her virginity right here and now.

Marshall moved his hips almost imperceptibly, but it was just enough to force the head of his cock into her virgin pussy.

"Oh Hanna," he breathed. His body was tense, completely controlled. "You're so tight."

"I'm sorry," she apologized. "I'm trying to relax. I'm really trying."

"You're doing beautifully." He smiled down at her. "It feels good on my cock, when you're tight like that. When a woman hasn't had a baby yet, her vaginal walls are much tighter."

"Oh." She nodded, feeling him pull back just a little. His cock head moved in little circles, hips moving just slightly, just the tip of him in her.

"Now a little more." He gave her another inch, the stretch of his head being forced inside stealing her breath as her body adjusted to him. He moved into her slowly, inch by glorious inch, as his hands cradled her face, one hand caressing her cheek and then running through her hair.

"Oh! Daddy!" Hanna cried out as he pressed deeper, her body tensing as his cock reached her hymen, pushing past the barrier with an impossible stretch and burn. "Oh no! No!"

"Yes, sweetheart," he whispered. "I've got you. Just breathe."

"Ohhhh!" She shook her head, wanting to fight it, push him away. But this was what she wanted, she reminded herself. This was Marshall, the man she'd dreamed about, the man she'd secretly wanted for so long. She wanted this. She did.

"Let's get to the other side." He kissed her softly. "Then I'll bring you more pleasure than you've ever known."

With that, he pushed in. The pain came, sharp and swift, but she bit down on her lip to stifle her cry. He kissed her lip where her teeth dug in, making her release it.

"Just wait a minute, let it pass," he whispered.

She opened her eyes to find him staring into hers. He kissed her again, gently, and her inner walls gripped his cock all on their own.

"Your tight little pussy already wants more." A smile flitted across his lips. "I can feel you squeezing my cock."

"Does it feel good?" Hanna focused her energy there, using her muscles to do it consciously this time.

"Oh!" Her stepfather cried out at the sensation, his hips moving, pressing him deep. "Hanna!"

"Is that a yes?" She smiled, awash with the power of it as the man bit his lip, his face screwed up, like he was in pain.

"Yes," he managed, his breath short. Then he opened his eyes to look at her. "Do you feel how perfect this is? How God intended us to be together this way?"

"Oh yes," she agreed, arms wrapped around his neck. "It feels so right. Anything that feels this good couldn't possibly be wrong."

"Good girl," he smiled as he began to move again inside her.

It hurt at first. His cock felt huge inside her, impossibly big, a steel beam trying to penetrate her flesh. Hanna clung to him, her nails digging into the meat of his upper arms as he pulled back and thrust, slow, easy, but still. She bit her lip to keep from crying out. Her stepfather whispered in her ear, sweet words, reminding her to breathe, relax, and slowly, she felt her body accept him.

With every thrust, he went deeper, each stretch building a heat that tightened her core. He propped himself up on his elbows, moving his hips faster, looking into her eyes, gauging her reaction. Hanna stretched her neck up to kiss him, wanting to feel his mouth, his breath hot. She could still taste himself on his lips.

"More, sweetheart?" he asked, grinding his hips into her pelvis.

"Yes!" she cried, lifting to meet him. "Oh it's so good, Daddy! Your cock feels so big and hard inside of me."

"And you're so wet and tight," he groaned. "Wrap your legs around me. That's a girl."

She did as she was told, feeling his cock shift, pressing into her softness, hitting something deep inside her with every thrust that made her cry out with pleasure.

"Do you feel that?" he asked, searching her eyes.

"Yes!" Hanna gasped, writhing, curving her back. She ached for more. It amazed her how fast it had all gone from pain to pleasure in the wet heated friction between their bodies. "Oh Daddy, that feels good!"

"I'm going to fuck you now," he said. Those words made Hanna's eyes go wide. *Fuck you.* They were so naughty, so wicked, but it felt so good to hear them from his lips. Why was that? "This is just how God intended it, Hanna. This joining between a man and a woman. This pleasure is the most perfect expression of His love."

"Yes, Daddy."

She opened and welcomed him home as his hips drove her against the mattress. She thought he was making love to her before, but now she understood his words—*I'm going to fuck you now.* Something else drove him into her. It wasn't just him. This was a pure, animal need, something bigger than them both. Hanna's body responded to his fever, meeting his passion with her own.

When she cried out, unable to keep her moans inside, he encouraged her noises, telling her to let it out, to tell him how good it felt.

"Tell me, Hanna," he urged, pounding into her, their bodies slick with sweat. "Tell me you like my cock in you."

"Oh yes, Daddy, I love your big cock in me!" she cried, flushing at her words, ashamed even now, but it felt so good to say them somehow. "Please don't stop!"

"You like when I fuck you like that?" He asked, giving her short, hard bursts with his hips, punctuating each thrust with a grunt.

"Yes!" Hanna's head went back and she moaned loudly. "Oh Daddy, fuck me hard like that! More!"

He moaned when he heard those words.

"Say it again," he whispered hoarsely. "Say it again."

She knew what he wanted to hear. Words her mother would never say to him. The woman wouldn't even open her legs for him. But Hanna would. Hanna loved him, wanted him. Wanted this.

"Fuck me, Daddy!" she urged, hips rising to meet his hard, hungry thrusts. "Fuck me until I come all over your big, hard cock!"

"Oh fuck!" Marshall cried out, moving even faster, if that was possible. "Sweetheart, Daddy's gonna come! I'm gonna fill that tight, hot little pussy with my come! Oh fuckkkk!"

"Come with me, Daddy!" she panted. "Oh God! Oh God! Oh God!"

It was the first time Hanna had ever taken the Lord's name in vain.

She came so hard she saw stars, beautiful white dots of light shooting before her eyes. Heat ignited her whole body, inside and out. She gave herself to him, her nipples hard, brushing against his slick chest as they moved together, both of them writhing with pleasure, each contraction inciting another deep thrust. Her skin tingled where they brushed together. She could no longer tell where he ended and she began as she let her body respond, finding bliss in each glorious pulse of her release.

"Oh Daddy," she panted, hanging onto him as if she thought she might fall off the planet if she didn't. "I didn't know it would be like that."

"Are you glad you asked me to teach you?" He kissed her forehead, his breath still coming hard.

"Yes." She met his eyes, smiling shyly. "Is that why they say that a man and woman become one? That's just what it felt like…

"Exactly right, my smart little pupil." He smiled back. "I'm so proud of you .You did so well, Hanna."

She glowed in the heat of his praise.

"When we've rested a while, I can show you some different positions a man and woman can find pleasure in. There are so many other things to teach you…"

Hanna remembered how he had tried to take her mother from behind.

"I love you, Hanna." He whispered the words as he kissed her cheek.

"I love you too, Daddy." She felt tears welling up. "I promise to learn everything you want to teach me. Just please, take me closer to God again."

"Oh my sweet, sweet love." He lowered his mouth to hers and Hanna felt him throbbing to life inside her once again, ready to take her to God.

"Daddy, the phone." Hanna's eyes fluttered as she woke, hearing Marshall's ringtone from beside the bed. Her mind was filled with the knowledge that her stepfather had taken her virginity, and her vision filled with him too as he groaned, waking and stretching to reach the phone.

She couldn't stop thinking of it, dreaming of him, even when they were in bed together. She couldn't count the number of orgasms he'd given her. She blushed when she remembered the way he'd shot his cum into her mouth for the first time, how surprised and clumsy she'd been, in spite of his warnings. The white, stick stream had splashed her cheek and neck and dribbled from her swollen red lips, her darting pink tongue.

But Marshall hadn't scolded her. Instead, he'd praised her for doing so well, even saying that she looked sexy with his cum on her face. Hearing her mother's voice come across the line made her freeze, bringing a familiar wave of guilt. Then, she grew angry. What right did her mother have to tell her daughter that this was wrong? That the pleasure of the flesh—bodies that God had freely given them—were a sin? Already, Hanna's breasts ached to be sucked, her pussy clenching at the memory of Marshall's hard, pounding cock.

"What's the matter?" she asked when her stepfather tossed his cellphone on the night stand, getting out of bed.

She watched as he stormed to the closet, throwing the doors open wide. Next thing she knew, he'd thrown his suitcase onto the bed, hard enough to make her bounce under the sheets.

"What's going on?" she cried, her heart skipping a beat as she waited for him to answer her.

"Your mother is staying at the church tonight to help the almighty Pastor David work up his sermon for Sunday," Marshall snapped, opening his drawers and shoving clothes into the suitcase. "I'm done. That man can have her. I can't stay married to a woman who only does what another man tells her to do."

"What are you doing?" Hanna stared at him, aghast, the words not registering.

"He fills her head with lies. As soon as I'm gone, you watch—he'll step into my shoes." Marshall snorted, half a laugh. "And he's welcome to them!"

"Wait... you're leaving?" She blinked at him in shock as he went to the closet to get more of his clothes.

"Hanna, I just can't do it anymore." He brought hangers full of clothing over to the bed, looking at her staring at him, sheet pulled up to her neck. "You're a woman now. You're old enough to go out into the world, to find a man to love, a husband of your own. But I... I can't stay here a minute longer. I'm leaving her. Let Pastor David have her. I'm taking that job in California."

She watched, bewildered, her skin crawling as Marshall packed his bag.

"Take me with you."

He stopped, staring at her. "What?"

"Take me with you!" She reached out to grab his arm, up on her knees now, her nude body exposed, but there was no shame in it. He'd seen all of her.

"Hanna, I can't." He shook his head slowly, his gaze moving down from her face to her body. "I..."

"Please," she whispered, feeling tears springing to her eyes. "You know I love you. And I know you love me too. Please, don't leave me."

"Hanna." He moved closer, reaching out to cup her face in his hands. "My sweet Hanna..."

"Please don't leave me too," she begged, tears falling down her cheeks.

He brushed them with his thumbs, searching her eyes with his.

"I do love you," he confessed, pulling her close. Hanna rested her cheek against his chest, feeling his heart beating hard.

"You said it yourself," she whispered. "I'm old enough. And I've already found the man I love."

"You don't know what you're saying."

"I do." She lifted her face to look at him. "I know exactly what I'm saying. You're the man I want, the man I've dreamed of, the man I love. I've loved you my whole life, and I will love you until the day I die. I don't care if it's God's will or not because it's mine. My own free will."

"And mine." He smiled. "All right, my love. You win. Go pack."

Little Brats: India

She was looking at her mother nude.

India had seen her mother naked before, but never like this. She was seeing her through her stepfather's eyes—not as a wife and mother, but as a woman, vibrant, alive, and terrifyingly sexy. Is this how Robert really saw her? There was such eroticism in the sketch, it almost pulsed with heat.

Cecile's legs were spread wide open as she sat, spine straight, on a chair, clothed only a pair of six-inch heels, her small, hairless pussy exposed. The erotic depiction of her mother, simple pencil on paper, made India's breath shudder on exhale as she turned the page in her stepfather, Robert's, sketchbook. Here was yet another sketch of the woman in a highly sexual pose, captured this time in various colors of ink.

India's mother had a dancer's body, feminine but heavily muscled, while still remaining thin and trim. She had a long neck and legs, but the shorter torso typical of classical dancers. Ballerinas didn't always have the most beautiful bodies, but in her stepfather's skilled hands, India thought her mother looked more beautiful than she'd ever personally experienced.

Cecile was a former dancer, her body slowly aging, but still, the woman had retained her figure, although her rock hard body had softened around the edges. India, on the other hand, had built a modern dancer's body on a well-muscled, proportional, solid frame. But that wasn't the only contrast between mother and daughter.

They were night and day.

Cecile sported light, blond hair with white, powdery skin and bright blue eyes. India's dark hair was a long chestnut, her skin a healthy tan, her eyes a rich coffee-color. While she actually took after her biological father, she had the same darkness to her skin, hair, and eyes as her stepfather, so much so people often mistook her as his real daughter.

She gazed at her mother's form, admiring each sketch, the detail bringing the suggestive poses to life. Anyone looking through—of either gender—would appreciate the artistry, the sex appeal in her stepfather's work. India looked at the next drawing of her mother, this one of her standing, bent at the waist, lace panties pulled down, stretched in a line across her thighs, her tiny breasts exposed, nipples pointing toward the floor.

India's brow furrowed as she flipped through the spiral bound book, looking through image after image of her mother exposed in a variety of poses. It happened gradually, but India realized that the further she got, the more clothes her mother had on.

The images started to change—a sheet wrapped loosely around her hips or arranged over her breasts—still arousing, always beautiful, but by the time India had gotten half way through the book, her mother was posing completely clothed. Flipping back to the beginning, seeing the dates below the artist's initials, India realized that her mother's willingness to pose nude had been short-lived after the initial date of their marriage.

Moving on to the next sketchbook, always impressed with the way her stepfather saw the world and reproduced it with fluid lines and graceful strokes, India discovered the sketches he'd made of his stepdaughter. *He's drawing me!* Most were recreations of photos. Many of them showed her dancing, capturing her, a moment at a time, in dramatic poses, arms stretched, legs bent. He'd captured all of her best moves. Her heart beat faster, fluttering in her chest.

India had grown up in the shadow of her famous, classical dancer mother. She had grown used to being invisible, even on stage. Her mother's presence and reputation simply dwarfed her own. But Robert—he had seen his stepdaughter as talented and beautiful in her own right. *He sees me, he knows me.* This proved it. It showed on every page, and she flipped through, breath coming faster with the realization.

As she got toward the end of the sketchbook, the drawings changed. In many of these, her eyes were closed in a peaceful state of slumber. In one, she was curled up on the couch, a bowl of popcorn beside her, where she'd fallen asleep watching a movie. He'd been watching her? Sketching her? The thought made her tingle with feeling.

In the next, she was in her bed, a small, sleepy smile softening her face. I wonder what I was dreaming? She thought, turning the page. Although she had some idea. She wondered if her stepfather knew she dreamed about him sometimes—in ways she knew she shouldn't.

In the next sketch, a thin blanket was draped over her waist, her small, round breasts glorified by the tight fit of the tank top she'd fallen asleep in. Her nipples appeared, slightly hardened, dark under the taut, light-colored material.

It was the most erotic image she'd ever seen.

And it was *of her.*

Not only that, but this was how Robert saw her. He'd found her beautiful enough to sketch over and over again, capturing all of her best features with the angle of his pencil, the seemingly simple shading of graphite on paper. He'd spent time, hours by the looks of it, looking at her, recreating her form with his talented hands

She lit up inside at this realization.

"India!" her mother called. "India! Dance class! Let's go! Now!"

"Coming!" India hesitated only a moment before secretly shoving the sketchbook into her bag.

Leaving her car parked on the street, so as not to wake her parents, India crept through the front door, sighing in relief as she got it to close with only the slightest hint of the lock engaging. Once she was safe in her room, she stretched her well-utilized limbs, giving her muscles much needed relief. Although no one in her family had been there to see it, she'd danced like she never had before. Not that she expected them to come. She didn't dance for anyone else anymore. But tonight at her recital, she'd done her best, feeling unusually confident, even inspired.

It was silly, coming home from a recital like she was sneaking in after curfew, but while she was expected to dance—to utilize her talent, as her mother would say—there was little praise left over for India. Cecile's interest in her daughter's talents had waned when the older woman realized their paths would diverge. India's focus on modern dance left her mother cold—and bitter. Cecile had always been far more focused on her own career than her daughter's performances.

India remembered her stepfather coming to a few of her recitals, sneaking into the back, bringing her roses and kissing her cheek with the admonishment, "Don't tell your mother." But he couldn't often get away from his studio, as he was usually under the calm, calculating and frosty eye of her mother. He, too, was expected to "utilize his talents."

"If you want a model, use one of your young whores." Her mother's voice cut through the silent house, harsh even at low volume.

"They're not my whores," her stepfather protested. "I sketch them. That's all, Cecile. It's art, not sex. And if my wife was interested in posing for me, I wouldn't have to pay someone..."

"I'm old and have no interest in being your muse anymore," she snapped. "I'm no longer beautiful that way. I see them come and go from your studio. I have eyes—and a mirror. I see the difference."

"Beauty radiates from within," he said softly.

"Oh, don't give me that." Cecile snorted and India pictured her rolling her eyes.

"It's true!" Robert insisted. India pictured him too, dark eyes flashing, passionately pleading with the woman he loved. It broke her heart. "Why do you shut me out? You're a beautiful woman, Cecile. It's only your anger that makes you ugly. Why do you close yourself off from me? You used to make my heart soar when you came into a room. My fingers would itch to pick up a pencil and capture your energy. But now? I feel trapped. Caged by your bitterness..."

"Leave then," she hissed.

India knew what was coming. She'd heard it a hundred times. Her stepfather said nothing, but Cecile couldn't drop it.

"I just want to remind you—our prenuptial agreement gives me the rights to all of the artwork produced during our marriage in the event of a divorce." Cecile's voice shook with anger. She didn't want the man anymore—but she didn't want anyone else to have him either. "I can make you a starving artist again in a second. Just say the word. I'll call a lawyer."

"Do you really care so little for me?" he asked, the sadness in his voice breaking India's heart. But it was a rhetorical question. They all knew the answer.

India heard the back door to their kitchen open and slam closed hard enough to send vibrations through the floor. He'd go to the studio, work out his frustrations with the fast sweeps of his pencil or paintbrush. She'd seen him do it before, mulling a piece of clay into something beautiful.

Often when they fought, he'd stay in the studio all night, working, then sleeping on the large model's platform he'd built with his own two hands in the far corner. She'd found him in there more than once, sad, bleary-eyed, a day's stubble growing on his chin.

The air in her room quivered with an eerie silence. She walked over to the drawer where she had stashed the sketchbook. Retrieving the drawing she'd torn out—and planned to keep once she'd snuck the book back into his studio—she got herself ready for bed. Lying under the covers, she held up the sketch Robert had done of his stepdaughter to study the curves he saw, the ones his black pen had brought to life with simple crosshatching. Was she anywhere near as beautiful as he made her seem?

She thought her mother was a fool. India knew, if she had a man like Robert in her life, someone who worshipped her, saw her as his personal muse, she would welcome it. She would never dismiss such a man, demean him, belittle him, refuse to pose for him, clothed or unclothed. If she had a man in her life who saw her the way he depicted in his drawings...

But he does see you that way.

She was holding the proof in her hands. That realization made her feel warm all over. Her muscles tingled, still singing from her performance, and she stretched, closing her eyes, letting that warmth lull her to sleep.

Hours later, her eyes shot open, startled awake to an odd sensation of being watched.

A man. There's a man in my room!

She nearly screamed before it registered that it was her stepfather sitting on a chair beside her bed. He sat, pencil positioned over the paper, wearing the dreamy smile that overtook his face when his work carried him away.

She had a thought—*he's sketching!*—before remembering, she'd fallen asleep holding one of his sketches. The one she'd torn from the book she snuck into her bag.

Where's the sketch?

She didn't see it anywhere and relief flooded her when she realized it must have fallen to the floor. As long as he hadn't seen it, didn't know she'd been snooping through his sketches. She didn't want him to find out she'd stolen his drawing of her. He probably wouldn't have cared, but she didn't want him asking her about it. She didn't want to tell him the truth—that she found it erotic, arousing, to know that he watched and drew her while she was sleeping

The lamp light was soft, low, probably not great to sketch in, but he didn't seem to mind. She shifted on the mattress, resisting the urge to pull the comforter up. The room was warm and she'd kicked most of her covers off, exposing her body in just boxers and a tank. Still half-asleep, she mumbled something, but even to her, it was intelligible.

"Go back to sleep, India," her stepfather whispered. "I didn't mean to wake you. You're just so beautiful—I had to sketch you."

She let her eyes fall closed, not wanting to ever disappoint him, but she couldn't hide the smile that turned up her mouth as the word—*beautiful*—flitted through her brain.

She marveled at the power of his words. Why should they bring such heat, spreading through her limbs like warm honey? She spelled the word out in her brain, *b-e-a-u-t-i-f-u-l*, a vision of white bubble letters that dispersed into a fiery rain. She probably would have dismissed those words from anyone else, but from him, they were like magic.

Slowly, she unfurled. Rolling to her back, she stretched her arms out to her sides with a sexy yawn. She felt as if she was literally glowing under his gaze. The scratching of the pencil on the paper was hypnotic, the rhythm changing from long, lazy swipes to short, hurried ones. After studying his sketchbook today, she could see her body forming on the page without even looking at it. Small noises came from his throat, subtle groans followed by short, pondering sounds he often made when thinking out his current project as he worked on it. His noises made her want to moan out loud too.

The eroticism of the moment took her breath away.

It wasn't long before her body was filled with the urge, the absolute need, to be touched—not just drawn. She watched him through eyes only opened to slits, through the thick, dark soot of her lashes. Robert had a scruffy, bohemian look about him. The rich, golden tan of his skin highlighted the course mix of chestnut brown, rich reds and subtle hints of dirty blond in his stubbly beard. He loved to work outside, bringing to life on paper to anything in nature that stood still long enough.

His pencil paused, the hand holding it rising to his chin to rub his beard as he tilted his head, his gaze moving over her body. Her skin prickled, a phantasmal static sensation, like being touched, not by hands, but by just a look.

India's eyes fluttered open and she met his gaze.

In that moment, which seemed to go on forever, they connected. India recognized the creative spark in his eyes, the longing and hunger there that only an artist could know. They'd always connected on that level. Her body was her instrument, the dance floor her canvas. She became pure self-expression, taking her body to its limits and back again. Robert saw that spark in her and fed it. The woman he'd married was a dancer, but Cecile studied what someone created for her, perfected the fluid movements of classical ballet, but the truth was, she didn't have a creative bone in her body.

India and Robert were exactly alike.

Sitting up and sliding off the bed, her body inherently graceful with every movement, she walked to where he sat. He looked at her, mystified, conflicted, rubbing his finger over the hair on his chin as she approached. Neither of them spoke as she got down on her knees in front of his chair.

Robert ran his finger along her cheek, their eyes locked. Rising up, still on her knees, she reached out to touch his face as well, her hand trembling along his skin. When she went to pull it away, he cupped hers with his, holding her touch in place.

Looking at the light sparkling in his dark eyes, his chiseled features, full lips, she closed the distance that separated them, bringing her mouth to his. What started out as a light press of flesh against flesh soon became a heated fight to get as close as possible. Feeling the fire of the kiss throughout her body, she longed to be closer to him, to finally have him touch her for real instead of just in his imagination, or hers.

Reaching down as his tongue invaded and swept through her mouth, she grabbed the bottom of her tank top to pull it off. When she pulled back to get it over her head, he opened his eyes, and something happened. His hand clamped down on her arm. Her shirt was mostly off, a rush of cool air reaching the underside of her breasts, and she froze, awaiting his next move.

"India…" He swallowed, an audible click. "No…"

She dropped her arms, the realization of what she'd done and how he'd reacted coming together in a cataclysmic rush of tears to her eyes. Her face flushed, she stood and ran into her bathroom where she stayed, letting the tears flow, but silencing the sobs burning her throat, until she heard him leave her room.

She heard him walk to the bathroom door and pause before he finally walked out. Listening hard, she heard the considerate, quiet opening and closing of the back door. Throwing open the bathroom door and racing to her bedroom window, she threw it open and watched him cross the yard, disappearing into his studio.

Then she heard the first crash from the outbuilding. Followed by another. And another.

Running down the stairs as fast as she could without waking her mother, she made her way to his studio.

She stopped short at the open door, seeing him throw a tin of paint brushes. The metal made a horrible clang, scraping to a halt as the well-used brushes scattered over her bare feet. Shocked, she jumped back to the grass outside the door.

"I'm sorry." Robert stood, head down, not looking at her. "I thought I was alone."

"No, I'm sorry." She stumbled over her words. "I just heard the noise. I wanted to make sure you were okay."

"You're sweet." He lifted his head to glance at her and her heart broke. His look was tortured, pained. "Always have been. I don't know where you get it from."

"Not from her." India glanced back, almost expecting her mother to appear like an apparition behind them.

"I'm sorry. I shouldn't have said that." He shook his head, sighing.

"No, I know." She watched his hands, down by his hips, clenching into fists, relaxing and tightening again. "She's my mother, I should know. She's mean, self-absorbed, full of herself. You're right, I'm not like her."

"No, you're not." He gave her a sad smile. "Sometimes I think you're the best of her. She wasn't always like this. I suppose she was always a bit superior, but once you saw her dance... I couldn't imagine having someone so beautiful in my bed. Guess it blinded me to everything else."

"I'm sorry she hurt you." She dared a cautious step back into the studio.

She glanced at the mess of art supplies scattered around his feet like broken toys that had fallen victim to a child's tantrum. Although, the man before her couldn't be further from a child. His paint splattered shirt hung loose, the top two buttons undone, giving her a glimpse of his chest. He stood there, looking defeated, in worn jeans and bare feet.

"Hey, careful." She saw the broken glass beside his right heel when she cautioned him, taking a tentative step forward so she could grab his fisted hand, tugging gently. "Let's go sit. I think we need to talk."

His head fell, but he let her walk him to her two favorite, old chairs sitting in a corner. They were old threadbare recliners, cushions sagging, stained with spilled paint.

She loved to come out here when he was working and sit in one to read a book or to study. She curled one leg under her as she sat, slowly, afraid he might bolt. She didn't want to scare him away, not now.

"I'm sorry about… earlier." He sighed, rubbing his fingers over his chin. "You probably think I'm an old pervert, coming in to sketch you…"

"No." She shook her head, denying it. He had it all wrong. "No, Robert, I don't think that at all."

"It's just that you're so beautiful, India." He didn't lift his gaze to meet hers. "I can't help myself. When you're dancing, when you're sleeping. Such innocence. I had to capture it. I had to."

"I don't mind," she reassured him. "I know she won't model for you anymore. And I know how much you admire the human form. The curves of the feminine…"

"Yes," he breathed, lifting his gaze, so much hope in his eyes. "You do understand. You always have understood me. I think my heart speaks to yours without words."

"I think so too." There was so much unsaid between them, so much they didn't have to say. "I'm not offended. I mean it. I think it's a compliment, that you'd want to sketch me. That you find me... beautiful."

"Oh India." He gave a deep sigh. "You should be showered with compliments. You are so talented, so incredibly beautiful..."

"You really think so?" she beamed under his praise.

"Yes." His gaze swept over her. "Too beautiful. So beautiful it hurts."

"Are you attracted to me?" The words stuck in her throat, but she managed to get them out. "Are you, Robert?"

"A man would have to be dead not to be attracted to you, sweetheart." A smile played on his lips.

"Then why did you stop me?" She kept her eyes locked on his. "Upstairs. Why did you stop me?"

"Because..." he hesitated. "Because I'm married to your mother. And even if..."

"Even if she doesn't love you anymore?" India prompted, putting her hand over his on the armrest. "Robert, I'm not a little girl, if you hadn't noticed. You know that, don't you?"

"Oh yes, I know." He looked down at her hand on his. "Believe me, I know. Every time I look at you, my heart swells. You light me on fire. I burn for you, India. It's wrong, I know it, but I can't help it. You have such a light in you, such beauty. I can't get enough of it. Of you..."

"Oh come on." India gave his hand a playful slap. "I see the models that parade in and out of here…"

"You don't see it, do you?" He shook his head, frowning. "Your beauty comes from within. You shine with it. It's not just your long limbs, your graceful body, although those are beyond beautiful… it's you, India."

"Me?" she breathed.

"Yes." He turned his hand over, lacing his fingers with hers. "Your heart, your mind, your soul. All of you."

"Robert, if you feel that way…" She looked at how his big hand, that talented, amazing hand, swallowed hers. "I still don't understand why you stopped me."

"Because I can't…" He looked at their hands, joined together. "If I ever saw you naked, India… I know I wouldn't be able to control the feelings I have for you. And those feelings… they have nothing to do with what a father and daughter relationship should be."

"Is that what we have?" She willed him to look at her. "Is that all?"

"India," he warned, shaking his head, trying to disengage his hand, but she wouldn't let him.

"You said you were attracted to me." She squeezed his fingers. "And after what happened upstairs, you have to know how I feel about you…"

"It doesn't matter." He pulled his fingers away, moving to stand.

"Wait!" she cried, standing before he could. "You said you wanted someone to draw."

"Yes, but…"

"So sketch me." She looked at him, hands on her hips. "Stop skulking around. Draw me."

"Please…" He looked up at her with pained, tortured eyes. "Don't ask this…"

"I've never felt more beautiful," she confessed. "How you see me…"

"India… no."

"Yes," she breathed, feeling her skin tingle at just the thought. "Draw me. Nude."

"I told you," he croaked. "I can't do that."

"Yes, you can!" She grabbed an empty sketch pad, opened to a blank page, and put it on an easel.

Then she walked over to the wooden base of the platform, grabbing a few of the pillows and tossing them around, arranging everything.

"India, stop." He came forward, but only to the easel. His hand gripped the top board until his knuckles grew white.

"You want to draw me." She looked at him, eyes blazing. "I know you do. Don't you understand? I *know* that creative side of you. I know what it feels like to not fulfill that urge, so everything in your life seems unbearable."

"But…"

"No *buts*. Draw me." She pulled off her top in one quick motion, tossing it aside.

The look in his eyes set her on fire. She heard him swallow, an audible click.

Her dark hair tumbled down to the small of her back, her pert, round breasts exposed as she pushed down the boxers she wore, stepping out of them and sitting on the pedestal mat.

Never taking her eyes from his, she bent one knee up, chest height, placing her pointed toe on the floor. The other knee, also bent, she let fall to the mat, opening her sex to him. Her hands behind her, supporting her upper body, she threw her head back.

"India," he choked out, shaking his head, as if to deny it, but he couldn't take his gaze from her body. He looked at her as if he could devour her—and she wanted him to.

"Draw," she commanded, giving him a fiery passionate look.

He picked up a pencil from the easel without taking his eyes from her. Again, like a ghost touch, everywhere his eyes roamed felt warm, tingling until her insides shook. Hearing the pencil scratch across the paper at such a frantic pace literally made her wet, her nipples pebbling, and not from cold. Feeling his gaze like hands roaming her body, she held perfectly still, except for the slowly escalating sound of her breath.

"Is this what you wanted?" she whispered, the intent look on his face making her tremble. "Is it, Daddy? Is this what you wanted all along?"

His pencil hesitated over the paper and then he nodded, but he didn't speak. Instead, he just went back to drawing, tracing the lines of her body, imagining her, re-imagining her, memorizing her with the strokes of graphite on paper.

"I wanted it too," she confessed softly. She kept her voice low, speaking as if in a trance, to keep from breaking the spell. "I secretly looked at your drawings. I saw your sketches of her. And your sketches of me…"

The slowing of his pencil was the only indication he gave that he was listening.

"All those sketches of me." She swallowed, remembering how it had made her feel to find them.

"You'd been watching me sleeping. Hours and hours, you watched me, didn't you?"

He nodded, almost imperceptibly, and she smiled.

"And what were you thinking about?" She bit her lip. "Were you picturing me naked? Were you wondering what my breasts looked like? If my pussy was smooth or furry?"

India glanced down, knowing she should keep still for him, but she wanted to see what he was seeing. Her sex was swollen, wet, her bare folds glistening. All because of him.

"I shave it for dancing, of course." She raised her eyes to meet his. His pencil was barely moving now. "Mother taught me. She said it was cleaner, better for dancing. But she did it for you, didn't she?"

He groaned, and she smiled, knowing it was true.

"You like it shaved, don't you?" India's hand moved over her own thigh, kneading her flesh. "You like how soft and smooth it is. You like to *see* it. All the pink folds..."

Her fingers moved to part her pussy lips and she saw his eyes light up.

"Would you like to draw that?" she whispered, circling her clit with her finger. It made her whole body come to life and she moaned. She couldn't help it. "Would you like to draw my pussy, Daddy? Every wet bit of my flesh?"

"Stop." His voice rose, a father commanding a disobedient child.

But she didn't. Her fingers slipped lower, into her flesh, into the deep recesses of her body where she could almost feel him entering her.

"Stop," he croaked, pleading now. "I'm begging you, India... stop..."

"Come over here and make me," she teased.

"India," he warned.

"Please, Daddy," she pouted. "Don't just draw me…"

She held a hand out to him and before she could even register that he'd moved, he was on top of her. His mouth took hers in a fierce play for domination and she instantly surrendered. With his chest, he pushed her down onto her back, grabbing her wrists in his hands, holding them so tightly that a throb of pain coursed through her, erotic, alluring as she moved against him.

She kissed him back, hard, forcing her exploring tongue inside. Their bodies tangled like their tongues as he wiggled his hips between her thighs. Releasing her wrists, he ran his hands down her body, making her come alive at his touch. Pushing up onto his knees, he ran his hands over her, molding her as she'd seen him do with clay.

"So beautiful," he murmured, his large palms running over her breasts and stomach until they came to rest on her hips. The skim of his rough fingers over her nipples made her inner walls contract and she moaned, writhing beneath him.

"Do you like me, Daddy?" She could barely breathe. "Am I everything you dreamed?"

"And more," he groaned, running those same rough fingers over her mound, rounding his palm over her bare flesh. His fingers traced her, every line and curve, exploring every inch. She couldn't stop the movement of her hips by the time he'd dipped a finger inside her, his others still roaming around in her wetness, leaving her breathless.

India rocked her hips up to meet his fingers as he slipped two more into her, gasping when he twisted them inside her. Her pussy throbbed with feeling, aching for him. She had never wanted anything more, but he was in no hurry. He touched her like he drew her, slowly at first, then finding a rhythm, faster strokes.

"Daddy, yes," she cried as he fingered her, thumbing her clit, strumming it, playing her. "Don't stop, please!"

"Good girl," he urged, looking down at her with half-lidded eyes. "Are you going to come for Daddy?"

"Oh God, yes!" She bucked up, her pussy clamping down on his thrusting fingers, drawing them deeper into her core. "Oh Daddy! Now! Now!"

He groaned as she climaxed, leaning down to capture her mouth, kissing her softly as she trembled all over. India realized, as she floated back to earth, that he was still fully clothed. And she wanted him. She desperately wanted to touch him, feel him on her, in her. But he wasn't ready for that yet. He didn't give her time to breathe before he lowered his face to her pussy.

"Daddy!" She twisted and moaned, hands in his hair, feeling his warm breath bathing her before placing little butterfly kisses on her mound. She writhed with the teasing effect of such blessed torture. Her pussy was still throbbing from her orgasm, but that didn't stop her.

She wanted more.

He slid his hands under her ass, pulling her up toward him. His tongue shot into her hole then, darting and licking until she saw stars. By the time he latched onto her clit, she was ready again, hips moving to meet the lash of his tongue.

"Yes, lick me," she whispered, spreading her dancer's legs wider for him, muscles taut. "Oh, that's so good!"

"Mmmm," was all he could manage, his tongue bathing her clit.

"Don't stop," she begged, rolling her hips, rocking against him. The scruff on his chin scraped her delicate skin, making her moan at the sensation. "Oh, Daddy, please, don't ever stop!"

"Nnnn-nnnn." He shook his head vigorously against her pussy, making her yelp in surprise. She was so close to orgasm, she knew it was only going to take a few licks and sucks to push her over the edge.

"Daddy, make me come!" she gasped. "Oh fuck! I'm going to come all over your face!"

He groaned against her pussy as she let her climax overtake her, hard. The feeling rumbled through her repeatedly until she couldn't take any more. She clenched her thighs around his head, hands fisted in his hair, riding the sweet waves of her orgasm.

When she released him, he knelt up, undoing the buttons on his shirt at a fast clip, letting the material slide down his arms to the floor. Her hands roamed over his arms, his chest, as he leaned in to kiss her. She tasted herself on his glistening lips and licked them, hearing him moan when her small, pink tongue darted between his lips.

"I've wanted you for so long," he whispered into her mouth. "I've spent hours drawing you, thinking about you, dreaming about you, wishing..."

"I wanted you too," she assured him, tugging at the button on his jeans. "I want you now. Now, Daddy. Please?"

He knelt up again and she waited, biting her lip, focusing on her breath lest it get away from her and she hyperventilated just as she was going to finally see his cock. He made short work of removing his jeans. Before she knew it, his erection bobbed in the air above her. Her hips bucked again, out of her control, but she was reaching for his cock.

She had to taste him.

"You want me?" He let her tug at him, moaning as she drew him closer to her mouth. "You want Daddy?"

"I want to taste you," she said eagerly, easing him into her mouth. His cock tasted salty, precum at the tip. She licked that off, watching his face as she pleasured him, loving the way his hand moved through her hair. Rolling to her elbow, she took him in her hand, pumping his length slowly in her fist as she sucked him.

"Oh India," he groaned, hips beginning to move, his hand moving down to cup her breast. She squirmed when he tweaked her nipple, feeling that sensation zing straight down between her legs. She was sopping wet, her pussy throbbing, still, wanting him.

Robert gasped when she slid a hand down to cup his balls, rolling them slowly between her fingers, feeling their weight. *So much cum in there for me.* The thought thrilled her and she worked harder for it, determined to suck him until he exploded into her hungry, waiting mouth.

"Easy, easy," he cried, pulling her off him. The sound of it made a thick "pop" and a string of her saliva stretched from her lip to the tip of his cock. "I want to be inside you."

"Oh, yes!" she agreed as if it was the first time it had occurred to her, leaning back on her elbows, letting her knees fall open in surrender.

"Are you sure?" His hands moved over her inner thighs, parting them further as he knelt between them. His cock dripped precum and saliva onto her navel. "This is what you want?"

"Yes, Daddy." She reached out and grasped him, squeezing, hearing him moan as she aimed him. "I want you to fuck me."

He shook his head, blinking fast, as he let the head of his cock fall between her folds, and for a moment she thought he was going to deny her. But then he gave in. She saw it in his eyes, felt it as he grabbed himself, taking control, directing the head of his cock into her. India pushed up against him, taking more than he offered, clinging to his back, her nails digging in.

He didn't even flinch. Instead, he sank into her, closing his eyes tight, mouth slightly open, face twisted, almost as if he was in pain. India found her breath, her voice.

"Daddy," she whispered as his eyes fluttered open and he looked at her. "You're beautiful. You're beautiful too."

A smile flitted over his lips and he kissed her, swift and hard, before sliding his cheek along hers, his stubble burning her skin.

"Am I dreaming?" he whispered into the shell of her ear. "I can't believe I'm finally with you."

"I'm yours." Tears, of both happiness and pain, stung her eyes as they started to move together. It was true. She was his. He'd possessed her for so long, she couldn't remember when it had happened, but it was years before this moment, this joining.

"Take me, Daddy," she urged, squeezing her muscles around him, hearing him gasp and moan in response. Her muscles—all of them—were tight and strong from years of constant use. "Fuck me, please? Fuck your little girl until I come for you."

"Yes," he growled, pushing in deeper and deeper as they literally danced with each other there on the floor, each movement, every muscle spasm, bringing them closer together.

"Oh God!" India cried, wrapping herself around him, arms and legs strong, meeting his every movement. He kissed her cheeks, her neck, her lips, murmuring how beautiful, how fucking beautiful, how much he wanted her, how he couldn't resist. Every kiss, every word, opened her to the feelings coursing through her.

Then he rolled to his back, taking her with him. India gasped in surprise, but she took it in stride as he settled her onto his cock once more, grabbed her hips and rocking her on top of him.

"Ride me," he insisted, looking down to see where they were joined together. "Ride Daddy's cock."

"Oh yes, Daddy, it feels so good!" She rolled her hips, grinding into him, rubbing her pussy against him, mashing her flesh into his. The head of his cock moved deep inside of her, hitting every soft spot. She put her hands flat on his chest and rode him hard, moaning when his thumbs moved over her nipples. He cupped her little breasts, teasing them, sending pulsing waves of pleasure straight to her pussy.

"Are you close, sweetheart?" he whispered as she bit her lip to keep from crying out. "Are you ready to come for me?"

"So close," she gasped, working hard for it.

"Let Daddy help you." His fingers moved between them, finding her clit, and she cried out at the direct pressure, the sensation making her quiver.

"Oh yes!" India squeezed him between her muscled thighs, her body going tense. "Daddy! Oh! Right there!"

"That's my girl." He watched her, his expression contorted with a feeling so powerful it rode the line between pleasure and pain. India knew that feeling, when you weren't sure you could survive such pleasure, but wanted over and over again, like flirting with a near death experience. "Come for Daddy. Come all over Daddy's cock."

"Oh!" She cried out freely, daring anyone to interrupt them like a petulant child as the contractions began. "Oh Daddy! I'm going to come all over that big fucking cock! Ohhhh!"

He growled and thrust up hard as she climaxed, her inner walls gripping him. She whimpered as she rode out the waves of heat, struggling for breath, fighting to remain conscious, her vision graying around the edges as she collapsed on top of him.

"Daddy's turn," he whispered, rolling her to her back, thrusting a few more times for good measure, making her pussy spasm around him again and again.

Then he pulled out.

India opened her eyes, her body still reeling from post-orgasm shocks, seeing him grab his thickly veined shaft. With a few jagged pumps and a low, unearthly growl of pleasure, he shot warm, sticky streams of cum all over her quivering belly. His body jerked and shuddered from each rush of pleasure. She watched, bathing in his performance, rubbing his cum into her skin.

"Beautiful." He smiled, leaning over to kiss her. "Someday I want to paint you covered in my cum."

"I like that idea," she agreed, scooting closer to him as he collapsed beside her on the mat. "That means you have to keep covering me in cum."

His silence made her raise her head to look at him.

"What?" she asked.

"I don't know if I can do it anymore."

"Do what?" She rolled to her elbow, looking down at him with a frown.

"I can't stay. But I can't go. I'm trapped. I have nothing."

"Don't say that." She touched his stubbly cheek. "You have me. I'm yours."

"You don't understand, sweetheart." He swallowed, throwing an arm over his eyes. "She owns everything I've ever painted. I signed that damn prenuptial drunk on love. She'll take everything."

"It doesn't matter." India felt tears stinging her eyes. "You can start again. *We* can start again. I can get a job, one that pays more than dancing, and you can work to build your stock back up."

"I can't ask you to give up dancing." He lowered his arm to look at her, shaking his head.

"I won't give it up, but I can find work that pays." She met his eyes, pleading with him. "Do you think I haven't felt trapped? That I don't crave independence, my own escape from this house?"

"Are you suggesting we run off together?" He smiled at the thought but India didn't.

"Yes," she said earnestly. "That's exactly what I'm suggesting."

"Beautiful India." He slipped a hand behind her head, bringing her lips down to his. She kissed him back, and when they parted, he gave a slow nod. "Let's do it. On one condition."

"What?"

"You let me draw you, every day, for the rest of our lives."

"I'm yours." She threw her arms around him with a laugh. "You can do anything you want to me, for the rest of both of our lives."

Little Brats: Jenna

When she found them, Jenna was pushing through the mess of folders, unpaid bills, and various office supplies in her mother's little secretary desk, looking for a few pages of mostly unwrinkled loose leaf paper to finish an assignment for her geography class. The stash of letters was shoved all the way to the back of the drawer, as if someone—obviously her mother—had been trying to hide them.

She recognized the return address instantly. They were letters from her stepfather, who was currently sitting in a prison cell, all of them addressed to Jenna's mother. She flipped through them, about twenty in all, realizing that not a single letter had been opened. But why?

Her original mission and schoolwork forgotten, Jenna shoved everything back, closed up the secretary, and took the curious pile up to her room. Some of the postmarks were months old, some of them from a year or more ago.

She'd always found it odd that he'd never written, never contacted them after he'd gone to jail. In truth, she'd been a little disappointed and hurt by it, but she supposed it was because the man was ashamed of what he'd done. Jenna understood, but even from the beginning, she had felt nothing but sympathy for his predicament, even if he had done what they said he did.

She sat with his letters in her hands, realizing he'd been writing to them all along, simply stumped that not a one had been opened. Jenna smiled when she thought about her stepfather. Scott MacKenzie had never been anything but good to them both. Tall, rugged, a real blue-collar worker kind of handsome, his smile alone spoke volumes about the kind of man he was. The owner of a successful building company, his was a real all-American-dream story of working his way from swinging a hammer to entrepreneurship. He had always been generous with his wealth, showering both her mother and Jenna with everything they needed as well as almost everything they desired.

His mistake, according to Jenna's mother, had been greed.

Scott had been caught using his company as a front to embezzle money from the retirement accounts of his employees.

She still didn't understand how the man who had lived with them, who had taken care of them all of those years, could be a criminal. Her mother talked about how he'd grown up with nothing, insisting that a taste of money had made him greedy, but Jenna wasn't so sure. The man she knew had been generous, but he hadn't been greedy.

But Jenna didn't have anything else to go on, except what her mother told her. She used to ask about him a lot, so much so that Jeanie, Jenna's mother, had finally snapped at Jenna, telling her to stop talking about him. Period.

Jenna knew her mother was stressed. What woman whose husband was going to jail for embezzlement wouldn't be? And when her mother was stressed, she ate. And drank. Jenna remembered, after her biological dad left, how quickly her mother had found and married Scott. It was like the woman couldn't bear to be alone. And while Jenna had hoped her stepfather would step in as their white knight, her mother's stress level only seemed to increase after their marriage. It didn't make sense. They were newlyweds, they should have been happy, but Jenna's mother had eaten her way to a size twenty-four and drank herself into a stupor regularly.

Not that Scott cared. He loved her, at any size, and told her so often. The man was a saint. Jeanie treated him like a child, she ordered him around, she told him what to do, she tried to control everything about his life—it was exactly how the woman treated her daughter—and none of that made her happy. Nothing made her happy. Scott kept trying, as did Jenna, but the woman was never satisfied.

She didn't blame her mother for gaining weight, but Jenna didn't really understand it either. When her mother was at her thinnest, people often thought they were sisters, even twins, with their matching red hair. Jeanie had that kind of baby face, and her family always remarked how much Jenna looked like Jeanie when she was that age. But having your husband arrested had to take a toll on the body. During the trial, everything in his name, from their house to their cars, had been seized and then taken away.

Jenna understood her mother's desire to sweep it under the rug, ultimately forbidding him as the topic of conversation, but it was hard not knowing the details of what had happened. It was even harder not knowing what was happening to him now. Just because her stepfather had gone away, leaving a hole in their lives, didn't mean she didn't still think and care about him.

She held the letters in trembling hands, realizing she was being given a chance at obtaining some answers. They'd been shoved to the very back of the old secretary and she was sure her mother wouldn't miss them—unless another letter arrived, perhaps. Then her mother would probably put it with all the others, and that's when she'd noticed they'd all been opened.

But maybe she could open them, take out the letters, and return the empty envelopes?

Jenna took the letters with her down to the kitchen. Her mother was still at work and she had the house to herself. She sat the kitchen table and, with the sharp edge of a knife, she opened all of the letters, careful to keep them in chronological order. The glue was in the secretary, and she went to get that, grabbing some plain white copy paper as an afterthought, taking her spoils to the kitchen.

She went to work, replacing the letter in each envelope with a folded, blank sheet of paper, before sealing the envelopes again with glue. She took a moment to admire her handiwork before returning everything to its place—knife to the drawer, glue to the secretary, and the envelopes, now weighted with blank paper, to the very back, behind all the office supplies.

Back in her room, Jenna glanced at the clock on her bedside table, seeing she still had a few hours still until her mother got home. Plenty of time to get to reading. She didn't know why she was shaking, except she knew her mother didn't want her to see these letters. And Jenna knew it, given the lengths she'd just gone to, concealing the fact that she had them.

But that wasn't the only reason. Until that moment, Jenna wouldn't have admitted, even to herself, how much she missed him. She missed his voice, she missed his smile, she missed his hugs. He'd been a good stepfather—far better than her biological one— and she had often wondered if they had meant so little to him, that he could just completely ignore them after he'd been taken away.

He didn't forget me.

That was the first thing she thought as she began to read. Tears came to her eyes as she read her stepfather's words. He said that prison wasn't all that bad—she was sure he was trying to mitigate it, even though she knew his was a white-collar crime and he was in a low security facility—and then he said the words that made her throat close up. *I miss you both so much, I love you. Tell Jenna how much I miss and love her too.*

He spoke about regret, about his sense of loss, and it hurt her heart to read it.

Then, in the next few sentences, everything changed.

Jeanie, I forgive you for what you did to me, to our life together. I've had a lot of time to think, and I get why you embezzled the money from my company. I remember every horrid detail you shared with me of the abuse, both mental and physical, that you suffered at the hands of your first husband. So, I can try to understand why you didn't trust me to provide for you and your daughter. But, I think I have more than proven that now, by taking the rap for you. I let you keep your life outside, instead of behind bars, to raise your daughter, why I rot away in this hell hole. I know you lost the house, but you still have my money, somewhere. When it's safe, I know you'll have it to live the life you want. I forgive you. I've said this many times, and I'm not sure why you don't write back or come to visit. Don't you think, after I destroyed my life to save yours, I deserve at least a letter, if not a visit?

Jenna stared at the paper shaking in her hand. It was her stepfather's handwriting, no doubt about that. But his words were so shocking to her, she had to double check anyway. She sat, frozen, her heart beating her in her chest while she fought for air. A rush of emotion surged through her, from fear to anger to disbelief.

Her body simply reacted. She broke out in a cold sweat, the hair on the back of her neck stood up, and an icy finger snaked down her spine. A little shiver turned quickly to shaking. Her vision blurred, a sudden dizzy spell making her grab her night stand to steady herself.

"Get a hold of yourself," she whispered.

When she felt strong enough, she went to the bathroom to splash cold water on her face. Then she went down to get a Coke from the fridge, grabbing a few saltines to settle her churning stomach. She couldn't believe what she'd read, but it was there, in black and white. Her stepfather hadn't stolen anything. It was her mother who had taken the money. And, apparently, she still had it.

She didn't know how long she sat there, looking at that first letter. She couldn't read on. She was too afraid of what she might find. What else hadn't her mother told her? The thought of her stepfather sitting in jail for a crime he didn't commit filled her with a helpless rage. There wasn't anything she could do about it, but her mother was the criminal. He hadn't done anything.

"Jenna!"

She startled, glancing at the clock, realizing only then how much time had actually passed while she was sitting there, in shock. Her mother was home from work. And she had all of her stepfather's letters in her lap. Jenna heard her coming up the stairs and panicked, getting quickly under the covers, taking the letters with her.

"Jenna, did you start dinner?" Her mother poked her head in, frowning when she saw her daughter in bed, Coke and saltines on the bedside table. "What's the matter?"

"I'm not feeling well," Jenna managed. That was true enough. She still felt sick to her stomach, and she was finding it hard to look at her mother at all.

"Hm." Her mother narrowed her eyes, assessing the situation. "Well, you do look pale."

"Just a stomach ache, I think." Jenna pulled the covers up further, closing her eyes. The letters were still clutched in her hand. "I'm going to take a nap."

"I'll go order a pizza, then." Her mother shrugged. "I sure don't want to catch whatever you've got."

"Mmkay." Jenna rolled away from her mother, a dismissal, and she shut the door.

Jenna's mother had always been a bit of a germaphobe and now Jenna was glad. She was used to taking care of herself anyway. Her stepfather, once he'd come along, had been the one who would take off work to sit with her, read to her, make her soup. At least those memories made the information in the letters easier to believe.

She knew her mother would avoid Jenna's room like the plague, now that she thought her daughter might be ill, so she felt safe to pull the letters out from under her covers. She wasn't sure she wanted to read any more, honestly. The truth was hard to hear. How was she supposed to keep this kind of secret?

But curiosity got the best of her and she unfolded the letter and kept reading.

I really want to see you, Jeanie. I miss you so much. I want you. God, I still want you. Sometimes it's all I can think about. I can spend all night just thinking about it.

Do you remember? The hunger in your mouth on mine, your hands, pushing me, pulling me. Are you shaved smooth for me, just like I like it? I know just how to make you wet. I want to turn you around and bend you over. I want the soft, round curve of your ass in my hands. If I had you here right now, I couldn't wait, I know it. You'd open your legs wide for me. I want to see you reach around and grab your cheeks and spread them. It's so pink inside, so wet for me. You're all I can think about. I want my cock buried in you to the hilt. Show me where you want it with your fingers. Press them deep into your cunt. That's my hot, wet cunt. I want to fuck you until you can't breathe.

I can hear the quivering moan of your anticipation, as you look over your shoulder at me. I can feel your fingers, finding the hole you want me to fill. My cock is so hard for you. I'd stroke it in my hand, rub it right against your pussy, up and down between those smooth, baby-soft lips. Can you feel the heat of it, the months of waiting, longing for just this moment?

How long could we stay there, savoring the moment, before I plunged the steel heat of my cock into you? A minute? Two? It wouldn't be long before our appetites took over. Maybe you would moan and wiggle back, or beg me, "Please, Scott, don't tease me, baby. Put it in!" Or maybe it would be me, grabbing your hips and thrusting forward with a groan, saying your name as I sank into your flesh.

It doesn't matter who, or how, I just know that we couldn't wait, and we wouldn't stop until we were satisfied. It would be a wild, violent, frenzied fuck—me pounding into you, our flesh slapping together.

And you would beg me to fuck you. Harder, faster, deeper, more! I couldn't get enough, I can never have enough of you. There's no end to how much I want you, and the moment my cock slid inside you, I'd never want to leave. The wet squeeze of your flesh around mine, drawing me deeper, making me groan and grunt against you.

I can see your ass rising up in the air for me. I can't help it. I'm helpless with lust, wanting you, filling you to your very depths. I'd grind into you, rolling my hips, panting and gasping and moaning as I fucked you.

I can hear you telling me, "Fuck me, baby! God, please, don't ever stop!"

But it couldn't go on that way, you know, burning so hot between us, for long—that delicious friction building, my cock swelling inside of you, your pussy clamping down on me with that velvet squeeze.

It's been too long since I've shot my cum inside of you, since I've experienced that moment that every man lives for—burying myself so deep inside of you that you can't tell where either of us begins or ends, that one ecstatic moment of bliss.

I want to take you, fuck you, fill you. I want to hear you say, "Come inside of me, baby!" I want to grip your hips so hard I leave bruises and shove my cock so far up into you that you can almost taste my cum when I shoot it, waves of white-hot pleasure filling your cunt so full you can't contain it. Can you feel it seeping out around the edges? I can feel it dripping down the weight of my balls.

So much cum in there for you, all for you. And I want you to take every last drop. I promise I'll save it for you, baby. I'll let you have it all.

God, I'm so hard now. You make me crazy with wanting you. I say I can't wait, but I know I will. I have to. I need to see you, Jeanie. Please. Write me. Call me. Come see me. Soon.

Jenna stopped reading, her breath coming in jagged gasps, tiny huffs of air like fire in her lungs. And those weren't the only flames that had been ignited in her. She knew this letter was private, that it was meant for someone else, but she couldn't help her excitement. So much passion, so much hunger. She had walked in on him, once, while he was masturbating—she knew just what he looked like when he grabbed his big cock and pumped it.

Had he done that, after reading this letter?

Her wet sex throbbed imagining his words were meant for her. Oh God, that was so wrong, but when she closed her eyes, she could see it. She could see him doing it to her, bending her over, fucking her, hard, stretching her, making her writhe. She was, technically, still a virgin at nineteen, but she'd played with toys enough to know she'd popped her cherry long ago.

In fact, some of best masturbatory fantasies she'd ever concocted had been about her stepfather. She would never have admitted that to anyone, but it was true. The man was impossibly kind and beyond sexy. It had proven to be a dangerous combination when she'd taken up the sport of masturbation. And for a while, she'd done it almost constantly—in the shower, in bed, on the couch late at night watching soft porn on Cinemax, but so often, it had been Scott's cock she was imagining buried inside of her.

She imagined him now, as she closed her eyes and unzipped her jeans, sliding her hand under the elastic of her panties to finger herself, circling her clit with her thumb. It was his cock she pictured, plunging deep inside of her. She clutched the letter in her hand, reading his words over and over, pretending they were for her. All for her. He wanted to take her, fuck her, fill her.

"Oh Daddy," she whispered, eyes half closed as she rubbed herself toward climax. "Fill my pussy. Fill your baby girl's pussy with all that hot cum. I want all of it, Daddy. Give it to me! Oh now! Give it to me, Daddy!"

She shuddered all over as she came, her body bucking under the covers, hips thrusting as if he were inside her, filling her completely. *Ohhh fuck. Fuck, fuck, fuck.* She gasped, clutching his letter to her chest, a slow, steady ache beating with the rhythm of her heart.

He was in jail, pining away for a woman who could care less. She'd stolen his money and tossed his letters, unopened, in the back of a drawer.

I'm going to save him.

The fantasy took shape in her mind, a small smile curling the corners of her lips.

The letter had ended with him begging her mother for a conjugal visit. He said he'd been on his best behavior and had earned it. She imagined the thrill of going into a prison and being locked in a room with a criminal, having sex when she imagined any guard could walk in if they wanted to. I mean, she'd seen it happen on TV shows, so it wouldn't be impossible.

Jenna turned off her light, tucking the letters into her pillowcase, before drifting off to sleep.

Waitressing took its toll on her, mentally and physically, but at least it helped pay her college tuition. Her father had stopped paying, and her mother said she didn't have enough to make ends meet. Of course, Jenna knew now, that wasn't exactly true. She came into the house, tossing her jacket onto a kitchen chair, her only thoughts focused on a hot shower and curling up with her stepfather's letters.

The rest of his letters were full of pleas, asking his wife to come see him, to bring Jenna. And then, there was the talk of sex. So much sex. The letters were sticky with her juices, she'd read them so much.

Jenna opened the fridge, perusing the contents, but a sound made her freeze.

She cocked her head, frowning. *It can't be.* But it was. It was her father's voice. Her biological father, Keith, hadn't bothered to come around much since her parents divorced. Not that he was much of a dad before that either. Mostly, he yelled and berated Jenna's mother, or talked about his get-rich-quick schemes. He was determined to strike it rich someday.

The sound of his voice in her house made no sense, but nothing surprised her anymore. Her entire world seemed to be built on lies.

She inched up the stairs, avoiding the creaky one, third from the top, creeping down the hall to the bathroom that adjoined her mother's room. She was hoping it would be cracked enough that she could listen. It wasn't, but she could hear them, her mother and father, their voices, not their words.

Taking a deep breath, she slowly, carefully eased the bathroom door open and peered through the crack. She had to stifle a gasp, putting her hand over her mouth to prevent any sound from escaping.

Her mother stood naked at the end of the bed, facing Jenna's father, where he sat on the bed. Jenna couldn't quite register what she was seeing.

"On your knees."

Her mother sank down in front of him as the man unbuckled his jeans. Jenna had never seen her mother humbled this way. Jean MacKenzie was always in control, always in charge. She'd ordered Scott around like he was a child—or, at least, she tried to. He'd quickly tired of it, but that was just who she was. Jenna knew she would never change.

So seeing her mother on her knees for her ex-husband was a shock.

"Do you want that cock?" Jenna's father pulled out his erection, shoving his jeans down just far enough to do so. "Tell me, whore."

"Yes," Jeanie whispered, licking her lips. "Please. I want it."

"You're going to get it." He grinned, inching forward to touch the head to her lips. "I'm going to fuck your mouth until you choke."

Jeanie made a low, pained noise in her throat as she looked up at him.

"Did it miss it, even when you were fucking that young stud?" Jenna's father yanked his cock away from her when Jeanie leaned in to take it into her mouth. "You did, didn't you? Did you think about me when you were fucking him?"

"Yes," she admitted with a vigorous nod. "I was only ever thinking of you."

"My God, you've gotten fat." He sneered, slapping her cheek with his cock. "I told you, I'm not going to be as tolerant as the gullible fuck you married. I want my wife back, you hear me?"

"I'm trying." Jeanie whispered the words. "I swear, Keith, I'll be beautiful again for you."

"He might not have cared if he was fucking a cow every night, but I sure as fuck do." Jenna's father grabbed his ex-wife by the hair and guided her mouth toward his engorged cock. She opened her mouth willingly enough, accepting his length. "You got your chubby little fingers on all that money and you blew up like a balloon."

Keith guided Jeanie's head, forcing her mouth on him, his cock sinking in deep.

"If I knew our plan to steal all that dumbfuck's money was going to cost me your figure, I would've kept tighter reins on you." He grunted as he reached the back of her throat. Jeanie gagged but he ignored the sounds, grinding his hips, eyes closing momentarily. He was clearing enjoying the sensation, maybe even the choking sounds coming from his ex-wife's throat.

Jenna stared, wide-eyed, aghast, not quite understanding his words, although they were beginning to sink in. Slowly. Like a dream.

"No one knows you like I do." Keith began to withdraw his cock, looking down at Jeanie with a half-smile on his face. "Do they, baby?"

"Mmmppphh." Jeanie's eyes watered as she looked up at him, and there was such adoration in her eyes, Jenna was shocked by it.

"Tell me." He withdrew completely from her mouth, his cock wet and glistening with her saliva.

"No one else," Jeanie gasped, drool sliding down her chin. "No one knows me like you. No one."

"Damn right." He grabbed his cock and smacked her with it again, first one cheek, then the other. "If you hadn't gotten us caught, we'd have his whole company right now. You know that, don't you?"

"Yes," she whispered, wincing as he smacked her face again with his cock, his hand fisted hard in her hair. "I'm sorry. I didn't mean—"

"You almost fucked the whole thing up." Smack. Smack. "And I'm going to continue to punish you for that."

"I deserve it." Jeanie sniffed, her lower lip trembling. She had her hands behind her back, Jenna noticed, although her wrists weren't bound. "I'm yours, Keith. Use me."

"I intend to." He yanked her hair back and Jeanie yelped as her ex-husband leaned down to look directly into her eyes. "You are mine. You will always belong to me."

"Yes." She nodded, although her movement was restricted by the grip he had on her hair. "Always. Always."

"I'm not going to fuck you." His eyes glittered as he spoke. "Not until you start looking more like a human being instead of a cow. Do you understand me?"

Jeanie nodded again, but no words came out.

"Until then, I'm only going to use your mouth." He ran his thumb over her lips. "I won't fuck that wet pussy you've got for me until I can see a gap between those fat thighs."

Jeanie whimpered, but again agreed with a slight nod.

"You're not to touch yourself. You're not to make yourself come. You understand me?"

Another half-nod. Jenna felt sick, watching this exchange. She couldn't believe this man was her father. He'd always been an angry man, and she'd often wondered why her mother put up with his temper, but she was beginning to understand.

"And if you don't get your body back, Jeanie." Keith snarled at her. "I'm going to take every bit of that cash—it's all in my name, sweetheart—and I'll leave you. Alone. You don't want that, do you?"

"Nooo." Jenna's mother howled. "I'll be good. I promise. I'll do everything you ask. I won't mess up again."

"Good." He gave a satisfied nod, moving both hands in her hair before shoving himself deep into her throat. Jenna winced at the motion, how rough he was, but Jeanie moaned, squirming on the floor in front of him, hands twisted behind her back.

"I'm going to use that fucking mouth." Keith thrust, shoving his cock deep into her throat, making Jeanie gag on his length. "Take it, you fat whore! Choke on my dick!"

Jenna cringed, but Jeanie actually moaned as her ex-husband fucked her throat, so fast and hard Jenna wondered how the woman could possibly breathe. She knew she should go, but the sight of it fascinated and sickened her at the same time, her father fucking her mother's mouth like that, her mother completely submissive, letting him use her.

"Ahhhh yeah!" Keith cried out, shoving the woman's head down to the base of his cock. "Take it! Swallow my fucking cum! Don't you spit it out! Swallow it! Swallow it all!"

Jeanie choked and gagged, but her throat worked as she swallowed her ex-husband's load, tears streaming down her face. Jenna gagged herself, involuntarily, and covered her mouth to keep in the noise.

While Keith withdrew, quickly zipping his pants and buckling his belt, Jeanie didn't move. She stayed on her knees, her face wet with saliva and tears as she looked up at him.

"My little cock whore." He tilted her chin up, pressing a kiss to her forehead.

With that, he was gone, out of the bedroom. Jenna waited to hear his footfalls on the stairs before creeping back to her own room. She sat on her bed, trying to make sense of everything she'd witnessed. The last shred of what she thought she knew about her mother and father had crumbled before her eyes.

They planned it.

It seemed impossible, but the proof had presented itself before her very own eyes. It hadn't just been her mother stealing money from Jenna's stepfather. This was something else altogether. Everything, from the beginning, had been a lie. Jeanie's divorce from Keith, her subsequent quick marriage to Scott. This was nothing but another one of Jenna's father's get-rich-quick schemes.

And it had worked.

Well, almost.

They were still planning on getting control of Scott's company, when he got out of jail. How much longer would that be? Jenna wondered. How much time did she have?

That night in her room, she took out the stationary she'd stopped to buy, and began to write a letter to her stepfather. She had only the vaguest idea of a plan, but the poor man needed something, someone. It was the least she could do. She started out writing as herself, telling him how much she missed him, wondering if she should tell him what she'd overheard. But what good would it do? She didn't have any proof.

She took out the first letter she'd read, the one that had turned her on so much she was forced to touch herself, reading his words over and over. Just looking at the paper made her wet now, Pavlovian. She'd climaxed so much to that letter, she was surprised the words hadn't been worn away.

Her mother had married him, but she didn't love him. She'd never loved him, never wanted him.

But Jenna did. She wanted him so much it was hard to breathe, hard to even admit.

She tossed aside the letter she'd begun, grabbing a fresh sheet of paper, and wrote:

Dear Scott,

I'm sorry. I'm so sorry. I know I haven't written, but I felt so awful, so guilty for what happened. I know what I did was wrong. Your self-sacrifice has made it even harder for me, knowing you're in there, and I'm out here, while you did nothing wrong.

Yes, I do miss you. I miss you so much it hurts. I've been so distraught, so afraid. I don't know what to do with myself, without you. I know I've broken your heart and that breaks mine. I know there are no excuses for what I did. I can only say I'm sorry. That you have forgiven me, that you took the fall when I didn't even ask it of you—I am so grateful.

I know I don't deserve a man like you.

Love, Jeanie

She couldn't find anything else to say in this first letter, but the man deserved an apology, even if it was a fake one. Hell, in her mind, the man deserved a medal. She longed to tell him what she knew. What she really wanted was to tell him how she felt. But she knew he would never allow anything between them. He still believed Jeanie loved him, had loved him all along. He was pining for a woman who had tricked him into marriage so she could steal his money. It made Jenna sick.

Those last words she'd written in the letter were true. Jenna's mother didn't deserve a man like Scott. Jeanie and Keith deserved each other.

And Scott deserved so much more.

She put the letter in an envelope, addressing it and peeling off a stamp to affix in the corner. Satisfied, she slipped it into her purse. She'd mail it on her way to class tomorrow.

Jenna crawled into bed, sliding her hand into her pillowcase to find the letters. She flipped through, finding her favorite, that first letter, when her stepfather had written about his longing, his passion, his desire for his wife. She could almost imagine it was her he wanted. If he only knew...

She skimmed the letter, his words swimming, imagining it was his fingers sliding under the elastic of her panties, circling her throbbing clit. He would touch her with such tenderness, take her with such rough passion. Not like that scene she'd watched play out between her parents. She shuddered when that image recurred, pushing it away.

No, Scott would grab her, take her, but he wouldn't humiliate or hurt her. She knew him, far better than he probably ever realized, when they were living under the same roof. She'd watched him come into the house all sweaty after work, stripping off his shirt on the way up the stairs to the shower, unaware anyone was watching. She had seen him stroking his cock on his bed while she hid in the adjoining bathroom. She had heard him cry out and shoot his cum so far it splashed the hard planes of his chest.

She could picture it all, every movement, every grunt and growl. Her fingers slid into her wetness as she played this fantasy out in her head, knowing it would never come true, but enjoying it anyway. She longed for him, to feel his hands cupping her breasts, rubbing her between her legs, even teasing her ass, making her yelp and squirm. She wanted his mouth on hers, sucking her nipples, licking at her aching clit.

And she wanted his cock. Oh, that beautiful cock. She'd wanted it a long time, but she'd been too afraid to think of it, too afraid to admit it. But she wanted him in her mouth. She wanted his cum burning her throat. She wanted him to drive into her, pounding her virgin pussy until she screamed and came all over his cock.

"Oh Daddy, fuck me," Jenna whispered, fingering herself, knowing it wasn't nearly enough. He would stretch her much wider than this. He would fill her completely. "Fuck me hard! Pound your little girl's pussy! Pump that cock in me! Do it, Daddy!"

She licked her lips, head thrown back, her clit pulsing with pleasure. So close now. So very close.

"I want you to come all over me," she murmured, imagining him between her legs, jamming his cock so far into her, the way she did with the dildo hidden in her drawer, so hard it hurt. "Give me that cock, Daddy. Let me make you come."

It was that image that sent her over—Scott rearing back, yanking his cock out of her wet hole and presenting it, slick and hard, over her belly. Jenna grabbed and tugged it in her little hand, imagining that first explosion of cum burning across her belly as she began to climax. The contractions forced her pussy to snap closed around her plunging fingers and she cried out, imagining the second stream of his white, hot sticky cum shooting so far it made it to her open mouth, giving her a taste, before he showered her breasts with more of the stuff.

"Oh God, oh, Daddy, oh yes, yes, yes." She shivered, her muscles tight, but starting to relax, even as the tiny pulses of pleasure continued. "I want you. I love you. Please."

She turned her hot face to bury it in her pillow, thinking about the letter in her purse. Was she really going to do this?

Her pussy spasmed again, as if giving her an answer.

Yes, she was going to do this.

And next time, it wouldn't just be a letter of apology. Next time, she'd find the courage to write a sex-filled masterpiece.

Her legs trembled and she was afraid she might actually collapse as the female guard searched her, the woman's fingers patting down over her breasts and then hard between her thighs, before moving over her ass.

Was she really doing this?

She was. She was about to see him again. Except she wasn't Jenna, she was Jeanie, at least according to the driver's license she presented when she arrived.

"You cut your hair." The woman guard noted when she glanced at it.

"Yes," Jenna had agreed, hoping she wasn't going to get busted.

But it was all going as they'd planned. Without a hitch so far.

She couldn't have done it on her own. She had enlisted the help of a more deviant mind than hers, the man who cooked at the diner where she waitressed. She'd concocted a different story for him, of course, as to why she had to see her stepfather, posing as her mother. Something about righting a wrong—which wasn't really that far off—and the man had agreed to help her.

She probably wouldn't have dared it, if their correspondence hadn't increased to a fever pitch. She'd become a slave to the mailman, intercepting letters from the prison so her mother wouldn't find them. Jeanie and Keith were seeing each other more openly now. Her mother had actually expected Jenna to be happy about it. That was a laugh.

But as long as Jeanie was distracted, Jenna could keep writing to Scott without incident or interruption. And she had. They had exchanged sexual fantasies again and again, increasing their output at a fever pitch. Jenna pleasured herself every night, often multiple times, reading his words to her. And they were to her, now, she was sure of it. Yes, he thought he was writing to his wife, but he kept saying how changed she was, how different, and of course, that was true.

Because he was communicating with his stepdaughter, not his wife.

The deception was hard to maintain, but she had a plan. It was finally coming together.

She had filled out all the proper forms, the background check was completed, and she'd practiced her mother's signature again and again. They made their "J's" exactly the same. Now it was time for Scott MacKenzie to have a conjugal visit with his "wife."

Jenna had thoroughly researched conjugal visits. She was surprised to find internet chat rooms about the subject, but now she knew that many female visitors were afraid of being watched during sex in the apartment used for conjugal visits that was housed within the walls of the prison. She learned that many female visitors requested the lights be off completely in the room, so no pervert guard could watch.

It was perfect. The room would be dark, and Scott wouldn't know until it was too late that he was having sex with his stepdaughter, not his wife. And Jenna had six hours alone with him—even if she had to pretend to be her mother,

"Well," the woman guard, looking down her nose at Jenna, made her feel like a common criminal herself. Her heart was beating fifty miles an hour and she felt the guilt like a weight on her chest. "Here we are."

They stopped at an unmarked door. Jenna felt her knees wanting to give out again.

"The room is dark, as requested," the female guard gave her a knowing look. "He's waiting inside. Soap, condoms and lube are on the night stand. You look scared, Mrs. MacKenzie. First time?"

"Yes. My first time," Jenna replied truthfully, although she meant it in more ways than one.

The guard only nodded as she opened the door. In seconds, Jenna found herself literally locked into a pitch black room.

"Jeanie?" Scott's voice, cutting through the darkness. "I'm here, baby. Reach out and take my hand."

She fumbled in the darkness, her knees hitting the edge of a bed, and then his hand found her, big and rough and swallowing hers. She gasped, despite her determination not to speak, not to give herself away. Not until it was too late. She had to make her fantasy come true, right here, now.

"I've got you," he soothed, tugging her beside him on the bed. She sank onto the mattress. It was springy and ridiculously thin, but it was a bed, and that's all that mattered. "You okay?"

His hand squeezed hers. She nodded, but then realized he couldn't see her in the dark.

"Can I touch you?" His hand moved up her arm and she shivered. "You said you've lost weight. I wish I could see you, but I know why you asked for darkness."

She'd been sure to tell him in her letters that, due to all the stress and her guilt, she couldn't eat and had lost a lot of weight so he wouldn't be expecting his well-padded wife. This was his "new" wife—svelte and trim.

"Are you okay?" he asked, his hand coming up to caress her cheek.

Again, she just nodded, but this time, he could feel it.

She knew, if she spoke, her ruse would be all over. She'd made it through the worst of the roadblocks, and now that she was here, on a bed with him, she wondered if a man could tell the difference between one woman and another in the dark. She figured she had all the biological similarities in her favor. At least, she hoped she did.

"I can't believe you're here," he breathed, cupping her face in his hands.

He kissed her, softly, lightly, and she let out a small sound, almost a whimper. *No words,* she told herself, as his mouth slanted across hers, his tongue dipping in to taste her. It was difficult not to speak, not to gush at him, tell him how she felt, now that she was here, in his arms.

Their breathing grew rapid as their hands began to roam. He was wearing something, a shirt, pants, something light and cotton maybe. A jailbird's jumper. It made her wince, but it didn't matter. She peeled off his shirt, her fingers fluttering over his chest. His skin was warm under her hand as she let it move down his chest, over his belly, gasping at the hard ridges of his abdomen.

"I've been working out." He chuckled. "Not much else to do in here to take the edge off."

She remembered him as fit, rugged, but this was something else altogether. She wished for light now too, so she could see him, but knew it wasn't possible. Her fingers brushed over his nipples, already hard, and he hissed when she gave one a light pinch before continuing to explore the hills and valleys of his amazing, new six pack abs. She drew an unseen picture on his flesh with one long fingernail, wishing she could see the light red scratches on his skin.

He moaned when she moved her hands to his thighs, nudging his erection on the way. He lifted his hips willingly when she tugged at his pants, yanking them off. His boxers too. She massaged the hard muscles of his thighs, from knee to crotch, until her hands brushed his balls. He sucked in a gulp of air as she slid off the mattress, her stomach clenching and fluttering, as she moved to nibble and nip at the thick mass of his thighs.

He let her do what she wanted, moaning softly but not moving to touch her. They'd talked about this in their letters. She'd requested that she be the one to initiate, to take the lead. He'd promised her, anything she wanted, but now his muscles tightened, his hands clenching, as she teased and tempted him.

She couldn't resist the urge to stretch her tongue out to taste his testicles. They were large, heavy, and she explored them, taste and touch, with her tongue and hands. She felt his body tense, knew how hard it must be not to move, not to touch her too. She nosed his ball sack, letting the hair tickle her cheeks. Gently, she sucked them, first one, then the other, enjoyed the noises, the animalistic, agonizing cries coming from deep in his throat.

She rubbed one finger along the tight stretch of skin between his balls and behind, making him jump and twitch. He tasted amazing, salty and male. He smelled like cheap soap, but also like she remembered him too. He felt like nothing she'd ever imagined, all soft skin over hard muscles.

By the time she grazed a finger over his erection, the skin tight, veins bulging, she was pulsing inside to be taken, fucked, stretched wide by him. She grabbed his cock, feeling it throb in her hand, and he let out a strangled cry, his hands coming to her head, holding her on him, not allowing her to move.

"You suck me at all, baby, and I'll explode," he told her, his breath coming fast. "I'm out of my mind with wanting you."

She turned her head, sucking one of his fingers between her lips, sucking him like she'd suck his cock, and he moaned at the sensation.

"Baby, I want you so bad." His finger moved in and out, mimicking sex. It made her pussy throb and ache.

She couldn't speak, but she could show him what she wanted.

Rising to her feet, still positioned between his thighs, she brought his hand up to her crotch. She'd worn something without buttons or zippers, at his request. Just a t-shirt and a pair of shorts.

"Oh baby, you're so fucking hot." He moaned as she rocked his hand between her legs. "I've dreamed about your pussy. You're all I can think about."

She whimpered when he pulled the crotch of both shorts and panties aside, his rough fingers parting her bare, smooth pussy lips. She was shaved, also as requested. They'd shared so much back and forth in their correspondence, she knew just what he liked, what he wanted.

"Oh fuck." He moaned, his fingers slipping into her. "Wet! So fucking wet!"

Jenna bit her lip to keep from crying out when his thumb brushed her clit. Her hips moved all on their own, responding to his touch. His hands were huge, covering her whole mound, and the other one slid up under her t-shirt, cupping her breast through her bra.

"Damn, baby, you've really lost a lot of weight." His voice was full of wonder now as his hands roamed. She let him touch her, explore, as he pulled her shorts and panties down. She stepped out of them, sliding out of her slip-on shoes. He slid her t-shirt off over her head, and she unhooked her bra for him, letting her breasts spill into his waiting hands.

"Come here." He pulled her quickly into his lap so she was straddling him. She felt his erection trapped between them, throbbing and hard, as he licked and sucked her nipples. Her hands moved through his hair, cut shockingly short, and she sighed and moaned at the sensation as his tongue bathed her breasts, his breath coming hot and fast.

"I have to taste you," he growled, shifting her onto the bed, so she was on her back.

Jenna cried out when he buried his tongue in her flesh, licking her from back to belly, again and again, like a starving man who had just discovered a buffet full of food. When he sucked her little clit between his lips, she gasped and bucked, her pussy pulsing against his tongue. He lashed at her cunt, spanking it with his tongue, his fingers finding their way into her flesh.

"Mmmmm!" Her hips rose, all on their own, her thighs quivering with need. "Nnnnn!"

They weren't words, but they were close. She wanted to call out, to say his name, to tell him to lick her, make her come, but she couldn't. Instead, she threw an arm over her mouth and bit down hard, sinking her teeth into her own flesh as his hungry, eager mouth sent her flying into orbit.

Her body jolted, twisting, his hands grabbing her hips to keep her steady as she climaxed, her pussy clamping around the plunge of his fingers deep into the pink depths of her hole.

Oh fuck! Fuck, Daddy, fuck! You made me come so harrrrrd!

She couldn't breathe. Jenna reached for him, desperate, and he leaned in to kiss her, tongue probing, forcing the taste of her own pussy into her mouth. It was heady and she gasped, her nails raking across his shoulders and back. She felt the press of his cock against her thigh and reached for it, hearing his sharp intake of breath.

"Easy," he urged, but he let her aim him, rub him over her folds, between them, up and down her wet slit. "Ohhhhh fucckkk. Easy, easy."

He was going to come fast, but she didn't care.

"Put it in," he urged, moving his hips forward. "I have to be inside you."

She positioned the head right at her hole, bumping her own hips up, and he paused only a second before pushing in, hard and fast, making her breath catch. She trembled at the sudden invasion. She'd fucked herself before with toys and even the occasional vegetable, but nothing had ever felt like this.

"I jerked off twenty times this morning, I swear to God, hoping I'd be able to fuck you more than a minute." He chuckled, taking a deep breath, and she giggled. "I may not last long. You're so fucking tight!"

Jenna's eyes flew open in the dark. Would he know the difference? Would this end things? But he didn't stop. Instead, he began to move, sinking into her flesh, his face buried against the soft skin of her neck, his breath coming faster and faster in her ear.

"Oh baby, you feel so good," he moaned, grinding his hips into her, buried so deep it hurt. She loved it, panting along with him, meeting him, rocking in the darkness. Her pussy welcomed him home like it was meant for his cock.

"Tell me," he urged, sinking deep into her flesh. "Oh fuck, fuck! Tell me you want it. Tell me you want my cum!"

Jenna cried out, clinging fast to him, unable to help it. He felt so good inside of her, taking her, claiming her with every thrust. She did want it. She wanted every last drop of his cum.

"Fill me, Daddy," she whispered into his ear, giving herself away in that instant and not caring in the least. Her sex pulsed on the edge of a precipice and he was going to take her there. "I want you. I want all of you. Come for me. Come inside me."

He growled and thrust and buried himself into her with a sharp cry. Jenna came too, the contractions of her orgasm transporting her over the edge of bliss. She cried out and bucked underneath him, his fingers digging into the flesh of her ass. She saw stars in the darkness and lapsed into a moment of nothingness. She was just a mass of throbbing bliss.

Before she could steady her breathing, before her inner walls stopped clenching him, he collapsed onto her. He held her tight, making it hard for her to breathe, and she reveled in the feeling.

What have I done?

She waited for him to acknowledge her words, cringing at the memory.

"You cut it shorter." He sniffed at her neck as he petted her hair.

He sniffed again, and she felt him stiffen. Now he would remember, make the connection that his brain hadn't before.

"You smell different." His hand moved through her hair, over her shoulder, down her body as he rolled off her onto his elbow. "Maybe it's just been too long, but something... feels different. You feel different. Maybe I'm going crazy, but this... it feels almost like the first time we've ever been together. I can't explain it."

"I can," she dared in her own voice. She felt him freeze as she said the words. Then she said it again, just to jog her memory. "Daddy."

"What?" He pushed away from her, moving to stand.

She sat up, searching for something to cover herself with, but there was nothing. Light flooded the room, making her blink to adjust to the change. It took a few moments for her vision to clear, to be able to see Scott standing beside the bed, naked, his half sheathed cock dripping with her juices, as he stood like a statue staring at her, open-mouthed.

"Jenna?" he whispered, horrified.

She turned to him on the bed, not hiding herself, but preparing for anything. Squared shoulders, stiff back, she faced him head on now as she waited for the proverbial shit to hit the fan.

"I can explain," she said.

He didn't move. He didn't say anything. His arms straightened beside him as his fingers curled into fists. He cocked his head at her, incredulous.

"Listen to me," she said, blinking back the tears that blurred her vision. "I'm the one who's been writing to you."

"You?" he breathed, shaking his head, trying to make sense of her words. "But Jeanie…"

"She didn't even open them!" Jenna cried. "She shoved them to the back of a drawer. I found them. I was the one who opened them. I was the one who read them. I was the one who cared enough to write you back."

"Oh Jenna…" His expression was pained, tortured.

"She ruined your life," she reminded him.

"She's my wife." He groaned, sitting beside her on the bed, head in his hands. "You're my *daughter*."

"She only married you for your money," Jenna blurted.

"Jenna, stop." He held a hand up, shaking his head, turning from her. She couldn't let this happen.

"It's true!" She grabbed his forearm, thick and strong. "You don't understand. It was her and my father—Keith, my real father—he planned it. The whole thing. He divorced her so she could marry you. Don't you see?"

"What?" He turned to look at her, confusion in his eyes. "What?"

"She embezzled the money and she gave it all to him," she told him. "That's why they never found the money."

"I..." He shook his head again, blinking fast, trying to absorb what she'd said.

"My heart broke for you when I found out," she went on. "I just had to do something. They destroyed your life. You gave up everything—your business, your family, your freedom—for nothing. She never loved you."

"But her letters..."

"They were from *me*." She reached out and touched his cheek. "They were all from me. I'm the one who told you how much I loved you, how much I wanted you—and I do. *I do.*"

"It was you?" He pressed his hand over hers to his cheek. "It was *you*."

She nodded, letting it sink in. She couldn't help her tears. They came unbidden and she let them fall, never taking her gaze from his.

"Oh, sweetheart." He gathered her into his arms and she let him, needing the feel of his warm flesh against hers. She sank into his full embrace. As she cried through continued whispers of apologies, in return, he ran his hand over her hair, soothing her by shushing her. Her mind went back to a time, not that long ago, when she'd had her heart broken by a guy and he'd held her tight, whispering to her about all that she was, all she had to offer that the loser couldn't see. She'd wanted to kiss him then as she'd looked up into his eyes to find them misty.

"I'm trying to wrap my head around this." He pulled back to look at her, smoothing her hair. "It was you who wrote me all those naughty letters?"

She nodded, flushing.

"I kept thinking how different Jeanie seemed." He shook his head. "She'd changed so much. But she hadn't changed at all."

"No." Jenna sighed. "They're planning to take your business. They're scheming, even now."

"Over my dead body." His eyes flashed.

"That's what I wanted to hear." She smiled. "You have to fight. You have to get out of here."

"It's not going to be that easy." He frowned. "I'd need proof."

"I can get that," she assured him.

"Even if you can, I perjured myself," he countered. "I admitted I did it."

"Surely you've already served enough time," she cried.

"I don't know." He sighed. "It will be a long road."

"But I want to travel it with you." She put her arms around his neck. "I love you. I've always loved you, and now..."

"But this is... so... wrong..." He swallowed, looking down at her naked body where she sat in his lap. "I can't..."

"You did." She smiled. "Boy, did you!"

"Brat." He laughed, lightly smacking her bottom. "Deceptive little brat."

"I did it for your own good." She grinned. "Yours and mine. You know that, right?"

"Yeah." He gathered her into him, rocking her gently. "I fell in love all over again through those letters, you know. I fell in love with..."

"Me." She beamed.

"Yes, you." He smiled. "You've given everything back to me, sweet girl. You've given me back my hope. My life. But it's more than that. You've given me..."

"Your love." She kissed his cheek. "I love you, Daddy."

"Yes, my love." He breathed her in, arms tightening around her. "My true love."

GET FIVE FREE READS

Selena loves hearing from readers!
website: selenakitt.com
facebook: facebook.com/selenakittfanpage
twitter: twitter.com/selenakitt @selenakitt
blog: http://selenakitt.com/blog

Get ALL FIVE of Selena Kitt's FREE READS
by joining her mailing list!

MONTHLY contest winners!
BIG prizes awarded at the end of the year!

BACK TO THE GARDEN

Discover the deliciously taboo lure of an incestuous siren call with four stories bundled into a wickedly hot anthology that's determined to keep it all in the family!

When Patrick's father went off to war in 1944, he told his eighteen-year-old son, You're the "Man of the House" now. Patrick's stepmother has struggled to keep them afloat, and he does what he can to help. He knows she's tired, sad and very lonely, but when circumstance brings a young woman into their lives for a brief time, it alters everything between he and his stepmother forever. Will Patrick become the real "man of the house" before his father returns from the war?

In "The Garden of Eden," Libby has lived her whole life with her stepfather, Ed, in a nudist colony. It's a very open, natural life, and they've never had an issue--

until Libby's mother, Kim, re-enters their lives. Kim is appalled by their living and sleeping arrangements and wants to take Libby away from the nudist life. Libby, still devastated by her mother's abandonment, wants to have nothing to do with the shopping trips and material things her mother is offering, but the longer Kim stays, the more everything--*everything*--becomes a greater temptation.

In "Lassoing the Moon," Leila knows she's always been closer to her stepson, Rich, than most mothers, since Rich's father left when he was just a baby. He's been the man in her life forever--but now he's really a man, and his coming-of-age is a test for both of them.

In "Lost Souls," eighteen-year-old Lily, raised by her fundamentalist preacher stepfather, Adam, isn't allowed to date or do anything against church "law." Asked to the Halloween dance by a boy she really likes, Lily defies Adam. But when they are caught in a compromising position by her father, what will her punishment and repentance be?

EXCERPT from "Lassoing the Moon" in <u>BACK TO THE GARDEN</u>:

 "I'm sorry about this morning," she whispered, looking down at the dark line of hair that started at his belly button and trailed down under the elastic band of his boxers. She grazed it lightly with her fingertip and found herself thinking about what lay beneath the navy blue material.

 He shrugged. "I should have closed the door."

 "Why didn't you?" She closed her eyes as his fingers moved lightly over her collarbone.

He swallowed. "I don't know. I guess I forgot."

Leila was trying hard to just keep breathing, to ignore the sweet sensation of his fingers on her skin, how it made her nipples tingle and harden. She didn't want to admit, even to herself, that she was getting wet, the gentle pulse between her legs turning into a throb.

"I didn't mean to interrupt," she murmured, teasing the waistband of his boxers with her fingertip. "It looked like you were...pretty close to finishing."

He cleared his throat, shifting his weight. "Yeah."

"Did you?" she asked after a moment, seeing what she was sure was a slow rise under his boxers as he shifted again.

"Mom..." he breathed as she snuggled a little closer, pressing her full breasts into his side.

"Did you come?" she whispered, seeing a definite tenting in his shorts now.

He swallowed and whispered, "Yeah."

"Good," she purred, feeling his hand slipping a little lower in her blouse. She knew she should stop him, stop herself, but she didn't seem to be able to. "I'm glad I didn't spoil it for you."

"You didn't," he assured her, moving his hips slightly, like he was trying to get comfortable.

"I haven't seen you naked since you were a little boy." He gasped when she slid one finger under the elastic waistband, tugging it up and letting it snap back. "It was kind of a shock."

"Yeah," he agreed, his voice lower, his breath warm and his lips almost touching her ear. "For me too."

Slowly, she let her whole hand move underneath his shorts, reaching toward heaven or hell, she wasn't sure which, but she found she didn't want to stop.

ABOUT SELENA KITT

Selena Kitt is a NEW YORK TIMES bestselling and award-winning author of erotica and erotic romance fiction. She is one of the highest selling erotic writers in the business with over a million books sold!

Her writing embodies everything from the spicy to the scandalous, but watch out-this kitty also has sharp claws and her stories often include intriguing edges and twists that take readers to new, thought-provoking depths.

When she's not pawing away at her keyboard, Selena runs an innovative publishing company (excessica.com) and book store (www.excitica.com).

Her books EcoErotica (2009), The Real Mother Goose (2010) and Heidi and the Kaiser (2011) were all Epic Award Finalists. Her only gay male romance, Second Chance, won the Epic Award in Erotica in 2011. Her story, Connections, was one of the runners-up for the 2006 Rauxa Prize, given annually to an erotic short story of "exceptional literary quality."

She can be reached on her website at
www.selenakitt.com

YOU'VE REACHED

"THE END!"

BUY THIS AND MORE TITLES AT
www.eXcessica.com

eXcessica's YAHOO GROUP
groups.yahoo.com/
group/eXcessica/

eXcessica's FORUM
excessica.com/forum

Check us out for updates about eXcessica books!

31927266R00112

Made in the USA
Middletown, DE
16 May 2016